"I'M HERE TO KILL YOU," SHE SAID.

Her pistol leveled, Fortuna halted a few strides from the men, and waited in wary silence while they slowly turned to face her.

"Boys, I expect you recognize the lady," Pearson said. "She's that marshal's wife."

"Widow," Stringer corrected dryly.

Benjamin, lifting his hands, grinned and wagged his head.

"Yeh, we know—and she's wearing a badge! I ain't never seen no lady lawman."

"You're seeing one now," Fortuna replied curtly.

"Badge don't count for nothing down here," Pearson said. "She ain't got no authority—"

"This is all the authority I need," Fortuna cut in coldly, moving the gun slightly.

"And you're aiming to use it on us—all three of us?"

"You're damn right. . . ."

SIGNET Westerns by Ray Hogan

(0451)

☐ **THE COPPER-DUN STUD** (125711—$2.25)*
☐ **THE RENEGADE GUN** (125215—$2.25)*
☐ **THE LAW AND LYNCHBURG** (121457—$2.25)*
☐ **THE RENEGADES** (119282—$2.25)*
☐ **DECISION AT DOUBTFUL CANYON** (111192—$1.95)*
☐ **THE DOOMSDAY BULLET** (116305—$1.95)*
☐ **LAWMAN'S CHOICE** (112164—$1.95)*
☐ **PILGRIM** (095766—$1.75)*
☐ **RAGAN'S LAW** (110307—$1.95)*
☐ **SIGNET DOUBLE WESTERN: OUTLAW MARSHAL and WOLF LAWMAN** (117441—$2.50)*
☐ **SIGNET DOUBLE WESTERN: MAN WITHOUT A GUN and CONGER'S WOMAN** (120205—$2.95)*
☐ **SIGNET DOUBLE WESTERN: BRANDON'S POSSE and THE HELL MERCHANT** (115910—$2.50)
☐ **SIGNET DOUBLE WESTERN: THREE CROSS and DEPUTY OF VIOLENCE** (116046—$2.50)
☐ **SIGNET DOUBLE WESTERN: DAY OF RECKONING and DEAD MAN ON A BLACK HORSE** (115236—$2.50)*
☐ **SIGNET DOUBLE WESTERN: THE VIGILANTE and THE REGULATOR** (124561—$2.95)*
☐ **SIGNET DOUBLE WESTERN: THE DOOMSDAY MARSHAL and THE DOOMSDAY POSSE** (126238—$2.95)*

*Prices slightly higher in Canada

THE VENGEANCE OF FORTUNA WEST

by Ray Hogan

A SIGNET BOOK
NEW AMERICAN LIBRARY

PUBLISHER'S NOTE

This novel is a work of fiction. Names, characters, places, and incidents either are the product of the author's imagination or are used fictitiously, and any resemblance to actual persons, living or dead, events, or locales is entirely coincidental.

For
Lois, my wife—and the light
of my life

CHAPTER 1

"Its Coleman! He's all shot to hell!"

Fortuna West, sitting at her husband Frank's desk in the marshal's office at Whitehill, Territory of New Mexico, came to sudden attention. A gust of fear swept through her.

The town's lawman, Frank West, had ridden out two days earlier with deputies Luke Coleman and Zeke Tyler to deliver a prisoner and a quantity of recovered stolen gold to the authorities in Santa Fe. While he was away Fortuna was following her usual custom of answering any correspondence that needed taking care of, and assisting part-time deputy Saul Harper in looking after the operating of the jail and office.

"Mrs. West—" a voice shouted from the doorway. "You best come quick!"

Fortuna was on her feet instantly, and heading for the street. Rushing out into the hot afternoon sunshine, she veered sharply left toward the hitch rack at the side of the jail where a small but growing crowd had gathered about two horses. Her breath caught in her throat. One of the horses

7

was Frank's chestnut. Over it was hung a limp body. Luke Coleman was being helped gently off the other mount.

"It's real bad, Fortuna," she heard a voice murmur as she hurried up.

She glanced at the speaker. It was Evan Crowell, owner of Whitehill's general store. His wife, Bettina, was her closest friend.

Steeling herself, she asked calmly: "Is Frank dead?"

"Afraid so," Crowell replied. He glanced to where Coleman was being laid on the dusty ground. "Maybe Luke can tell us what happened."

Fortuna, shock turning her mute and remote, nodded woodenly, and followed the merchant a half dozen steps to where the deputy lay. It was a wonder the man was still alive, she realized, giving him a quick, appraising look. He was badly shot up, as someone had noted—there being three, perhaps four bullet wounds visible—and having had considerable firsthand experience with such during the ten years she had been married to, and worked with, Frank West in his capacity as lawman, Fortuna could imagine the hell Coleman must have gone through in making the long ride back to the settlement.

"Was an ambush," Coleman was saying in a faltering voice. "Pearson had them friends of his'n—Stringer and Tom Benjamin—waiting for us at Haystack Canyon."

"Haystack Canyon!" someone in the crowd

echoed. "What was you all doing that far east of the trail?"

"Was that—that damned Zeke Tyler. Talked the marshal into making camp there. Zeke was one of them. He went and throwed in with Pearson and the others."

A complete silence, broken only by the distant barking of a dog and the weary shifting of the horses, followed Luke's labored words.

Frank's death was now beginning to register fully on Fortuna's consciousness. It seemed impossible that it could be true, yet that fact was before her. Through the years she had endeavored to prepare herself for such a moment, knowing all along, deep inside her, that the time would most likely come when death at the hands of some outlaw would take him from her. A good, honest, straightforward man who believed the law must be upheld at any and all costs, it was inevitable a bullet would eventually overtake him.

"Last I seen of them," she heard Coleman say in answer to a question put to him, "they was heading east—like they was going to Texas."

"Mrs. West, you want me to look after the marshal?"

Corey Glenn, the town's combination undertaker and cabinetmaker, was at her shoulder. His voice was low and respectful. Fortuna nodded.

"If you'll drop by the house after a bit I'll give you some clothes—his best suit and a new shirt."

"Yes'm. Will the burying be in the morning?"

"In the morning—"

"They opened up on Frank and me just as we was climbing off our horses," Coleman's dragging voice came to Fortuna. "We didn't have no chance to draw iron."

Whitehill's medical man, Doc Rowe, had arrived, and was now hunched beside the deputy, she saw. The physician glanced about at the faces turned to him, shook his head.

"No point in moving Luke. Just cause him more pain."

Despite the driving summer heat a coldness was now filling Fortuna West. The initial, deadening shock with its numbing grief was passing, and now a sullen anger was taking over. A large, well-built, strong woman, she pushed forward abruptly through the crowd, and knelt beside Coleman.

"Luke," she said, cutting in on a question being put to the dying lawman by Jake Dietrich, one of Whitehill's town councilmen. "You said Pearson and the others headed east for Texas—they mention any town?"

Coleman stared up at Fortuna. His features were slack, and his eyes had taken on a dullness. "I'm right sorry, Mrs. West. Just wished it hadn't gone and happened."

"No fault of yours," Fortuna said, her voice unnecessarily crisp, considering the man's condition. And then as if realizing, she softened her tone and added: "I know you did all you could, Luke."

"They went and left us both for dead—only I

weren't clean gone," the deputy continued wearily. "Soon's they rode off I drug myself over to where Frank was laying. Got him up on his horse, tied him good so's he couldn't fall off. Then I climbed up onto mine."

"Some sort of miracle, that," Doc Rowe said, admiringly.

"Then I lit out for here," Coleman rambled on. "Was mighty slow going—Haystack Canyon's a far piece—specially when a man ain't sure of where he is or what's going on around him."

"Like Doc says, it's a miracle you made it at all," Jake Dietrich commented.

"Guess I just figured I had to," Coleman said, and turning his head to one side, coughed raggedly. That over, he brought his wavering attention back to Fortuna.

"I ain't thinking so good, Mrs. West, but I reckon Pearson and them headed for some town in Texas—close by. Would be wanting to blow some of that gold—gambling, and drinking, and womaning."

"Twenty thousand dollars in double eagles," a man in the crowd said in an awed tone. "Fellow could sure have himself one hell of a big time if—"

The speaker broke off as if silenced by someone in the gathering. Two more of the town's council had arrived on the scene—Max Springfield, who owned the gun and saddle shop, and Joe Payne, the feed-store merchant. All members of the governing body were now present. They listened quietly as Crowell gave them details of the incident. When he had finished Payne turned to Rowe.

"Hadn't we better get Luke over to your office?"

Rowe shrugged and bent over the deputy. Overhead, in the vivid blue of the hot, cloudless sky crows were straggling noisily by on their way to the trees growing along Jimson's Creek where they would roost for the night.

"Won't be necessary," the physician said in a resigned voice. "He's dead. Some of you take him down to Corey Glenn's."

Several men stepped forward to comply. Joe Payne pulled off his hat, and turned to Fortuna.

"Can't tell you how sorry I am about this. Frank was a good man—and a fine lawman—one of the best, in fact. It's too late to make up a posse and go after that bunch, but me and the council will get off a letter on the next stage asking the sheriff and the U.S. marshal to both take a hand in running down those killers."

"That'll take a week, maybe more," Fortuna said, frowning. "By then Red Pearson and the rest of them can be hundreds of miles away."

Dietrich nodded agreement. "Ain't no denying that! Maybe one of these days we'll have telegraph service, and—"

"Forget the letter," Fortuna cut in brusquely. "I'm not waiting for the sheriff or the U.S. marshal—I'm going after them myself."

A murmur of surprise ran through the crowd. Jake Dietrich rubbed at his jaw, and glanced about uncertainly. It was Payne who found voice.

"That's fool talk, Fortuna! No woman can go out looking for a bunch of hardcase killers like them!"

"I can—and will," Fortuna said quietly. "I can handle myself, Joe—and you damn well know it! I've been with Frank often enough to know the ropes."

"But you—you're a woman—and you'll be going up against all kinds of riffraff, not to mention the likes of Red Pearson, and them others."

"Expect I'm as good with a six-shooter and a rifle as they are. And I can track better'n most—better than an Indian even, Frank once told me."

"But to go after them alone," Dietrich protested, lifting his hands in a gesture of despair. "It'll be a tough, risky job for an experienced lawman, and you, a woman—"

"Jake," Fortuna broke in, shaking her head, "I'm tired of hearing about me being a woman! I am—but that doesn't make a bit of difference—and I don't aim to let those killers get away with murdering my husband—and Luke, and that's just what they'll do if we wait around for the U.S. marshal and the sheriff to get on the job!"

"I reckon she's right," Evan Crowell said. "It's just that I ain't so sure she—"

"I'll be pulling out soon as Frank's buried, and I can get some gear together. Means tomorrow morning, late probably. Now, I'll need to be commissioned a deputy so that whatever I do will be according to law."

Fortuna paused, awaited the reaction to her

words. Dietrich was thoughtful for several moments, then again lifting his hands, allowed them to fall to his sides helplessly.

"All right—all right! But you best remember that this is all your doing, Fortuna! Now, right here before God, and everybody that can hear my voice—as head of the town council—I commission you a deputy marshal. But only on one condition."

Fortuna stared at Dietrich suspiciously. "Condition? What condition?"

"That you take Saul Harper along. I ain't turning you loose out there unless you've got a man with you. Just don't want it on my conscience if things don't turn out right."

"Jake's right," Evan Crowell agreed. "For your own safety you need a man with you."

Saul Harper . . . Fortuna doubted the part-time deputy would prove of much help in a fight, but she reckoned he could serve the purpose—that of being the male companion they seemed to think she should have. Anyway, if it would satisfy Dietrich and the town council, she was willing to go along with the idea.

"Whatever you say," she said, and glancing around located Harper in the crowd. The body of Luke Coleman had been carried away, and the gathering was now much smaller.

"Get your gear together—I'll take care of the pack horse and trail grub," she said briskly. "We'll leave in the morning after the funeral."

CHAPTER 2

"Are you going to try and make yourself look like a man?" Bettina Crowell asked.

It was evening, and Fortuna, having spent an hour or more sitting beside Frank's coffin in the funeral room of Corey Glenn's place during which she, in private, let her grief have its way, was now in the bedroom of the small house she and her husband had occupied ever since they lived in Whitehill. She hadn't felt like eating, had only picked at the supper Bettina had brought to her.

The house seemed strangely hushed to Fortuna, even with her closest friend there with her. Always before Frank's presence could be felt even though he might be far away on lawman's business of some sort. The personal things of his, the smell of his pipe tobacco, the worn brush jacket hanging in a corner that he steadfastly refused to throw away—all exuded a warmness reminding her of his being. But that had ended, no longer existed.

The change, she supposed, had come about simply because she had finally accepted the fact that he would not return, that she would never again see him stride along the walk, his big frame filling the doorway, and enter the house. The loneliness of the realization cut deep into her heart, and she knew it would remain there for a long time—perhaps forever.

And the people of the town dropping by to express their condolences didn't help matters any. She appreciated their thoughtfulness, but each visit only raked open the wound caused by Frank's death, and renewed her throbbing grief.

"Fortuna? I asked you if—"

At Bettina's words Fortuna shook her head. "No, I don't plan to," she said, turning away from the closet where she had been selecting the clothing she intended to wear—a pair of pants, once Frank's but altered to fit her more comfortably, and that she used when they went on hunting trips or planned to be in the saddle for any length of time; a button shirt, also once Frank's; the fringed doeskin jacket he had bought her from a Kiowa Indian; boots; a brown, flat crowned hat; red bandanna; and a change of underwear.

Bettina Crowell, her large, sad eyes reflecting the grief she felt for her friend, plucked at the edge of the apron she was wearing.

"Just as well," she murmured. "Is there anything of mine or Evan's that you want?"

Fortuna, reaching up to the top shelf of the closet, obtained her gun belt, holster, and pistol—a .44 caliber weapon chambered to use the same cartridge as her rifle. The derringer Frank had given her to carry when occasion warranted she passed up, but she did add the keen-edged skinning knife and its sheath on the bed alongside the other articles.

"Thank you, no—I have everything I need. Frank fixed me up with an outfit years ago."

"What about tomorrow—the funeral, I mean? Can we do anything?"

Fortuna gave that a few moments' thought, and once again shook her head. "Everything has been taken care of, thanks to Evan and some of the others."

"You still plan to leave right after the service is over?"

"Just as soon as it's finished—I'll be dressed and ready to ride out. I've told Saul Harper to be ready, too."

Bettina, toying now with the lace fringe of her bodice, glanced through the open window. Full darkness had set in, and the soft, warm night was filled with the overpowering sweetness of a honeysuckle growing close by.

"It's not for me to be saying, Fortuna," Bettina began slowly, "but do you think that's wise—just leave town as soon as Frank's buried? People will talk—"

"I don't give a damn what people will do!" Fortuna snapped, suddenly angry. "I only know I have to get on the trail of those—those killers fast, and bring them back here to hang."

"I hope you can," Bettina said. A short, heavy-set woman with graying hair and placid blue eyes, she considered Fortuna West quietly. Then, "I'm sure that's a reason for your being in a hurry, but I wonder if there isn't more to it."

"Meaning?"

"You probably have a need to do something, to get away from here, keep busy so you won't have time to think about Frank."

"Maybe, but I'll always be thinking about him, remembering the things we did, all the fun we had. We had a fine life together, Bett. It was just too good to last, I guess."

"Seems to work out that way sometimes. I often wondered how much you worried about him, being a lawman and all that. There was always a chance that he—that he—"

"That he'd get himself killed?" Fortuna finished. "It bothered me, all right, and it was something I had to learn to live with. But he never thought much about it. He believed in himself and his ability to do the job he had taken an oath to fulfill. And there was something else he believed in—that keeping law and order was what God put him on this earth to do."

Bettina Crowell lowered her head, dabbing at her eyes with a handkerchief. "I can't help thinking of what a terrible loss it is. A good man like him getting shot down while hundreds of worthless saddle bums and outlaws go on living. I find it hard to understand how things like that can happen."

"Found myself wondering the same thing," Fortuna replied, her voice strong and steady. "This is one time the outlaws won't get away with their killing! Every last one of them will pay with his life for murdering Frank!"

As she spoke Fortuna West's voice had taken on a grimness. Standing as she was before the window, staring out into the shadow-filled moonlight, she made a strong, resolute shape.

Taller than average for her sex, she had wide shoulders and a lean but solid body. Generally terming herself a washed-out redhead, she had level blue eyes, a handsome if not pretty face, and a wealth of red hair. There was a look of capability to her, and it was entirely possible she could pass for a man if it became necessary.

"Will you kill Pearson or any of the others if you have to?" Bettina asked, hesitantly.

Fortuna's reply was immediate and inflexible. "Of course! Frank always said it was up to the outlaw whether he lived or died. If Pearson, or any of the others, are willing to throw down their guns and become my prisoners, then all well and good. If they choose instead to fight me, I'll do my best to kill them—and not be one bit sorry."

Bettina shuddered. "I've never heard you talk like this before—so hard, so matter-of-fact about things."

"Frank was never murdered before," Fortuna said dryly. "I'm living in a whole new world now, one where it will be kill or be killed—and I don't figure to let the last happen—leastwise not until I've made Red Pearson, and Tom Benjamin, and

Ike Stringer—and that dirty little double-crossing deputy, Zeke Tyler—pay for what they did."

"And then after that?" Bettina pressed gently. Faint strains of piano music were drifting in, coming from one of the town's saloons—an indication that regardless of tragedy life went on.

"I've not given that any thought," Fortuna answered. "I'm taking things one day at a time, and I'll decide on that when I get back—if I get back."

She turned and glanced to the door. A knock came, and then the panel opened to admit Evan Crowell. Smiling slightly, he nodded to Fortuna, and crossed to where his wife sat.

"I see you're about ready," he said, looking at the assemblage of items on the bed. "Are you sure about this, Fortuna?"

"I am—"

"Well, I'm not sure Frank would be in favor of it."

"He believed in the law—and I'm simply upholding it just as he would do."

"But Frank was a man—an experienced lawman," Crowell said with a shake of his head. "Fortuna, there's a lot of talk going around town about you doing this—and plenty of betting, too."

"Betting?"

"Yes, they're laying odds that you'll come crawling back after a couple of days, ready to quit, and turn the job over to the U.S. marshal or some deputy from the sheriff's office, let a regular lawman do the hunting down of those outlaws."

Fortuna smiled tightly. "You can make yourself some money, Evan, if you take a few of those bets. I'll be back all right, but I won't be crawling. I'll be bringing those killers with me—either dead or alive. . . . Now, I have to finish getting things ready, and then grab a bit of sleep. Thanks again to both of you for all you've done. I'll see you again in the morning—at the funeral."

Bettina Crowell got to her feet, and with her husband, crossed to the door. She paused. "Are you certain you don't want me to stay with you?"

"I'm sure. . . . Good night."

"Good night," the Crowells said in unison, and continued on their way.

"Something bad keeps nagging at me about this here little sashay we're making," Saul Harper said shortly after they had ridden out of the settlement. "There's four of them, and only two of us—and one of us is—"

Fortuna had just taken a final look at the small, tree-bordered cemetery west of Whitehill. The crowd attending burial service for Frank West had disappeared, and now only the lonely figure of the sexton at work filling in the grave was to be seen.

"A woman—that what you're trying to say?" she finished, noting the deputy's hesitation.

"Well, yeh, I reckon that's it. Just don't seem fitting for a woman to be doing what you're aiming to."

Fortuna looked ahead, ignoring the faint stir of

anger that she felt. She was pleased that they had gotten away early, and were now well on their way to Haystack Canyon where she hoped to pick up the trail of the outlaws.

"What difference does it make?" she said, now shifting her attention to the pack horse at the end of a short rope, trailing behind her. She had come well provisioned and equipped for the trip, uncertain, of course, whether she was in for a long chase or not.

"I can shoot better than most men—and I can draw my pistol faster than a lot of them—thanks to my husband."

Harper nodded morosely. Just turned forty, he was of average build, had muddy brown eyes and thinning, dark hair. A secret admirer of Fortuna, he had always kept the fact to himself, standing as he did a bit in awe of her.

"Yeh, I know that, but it just don't seem right—a woman out doing what rightfully a man's supposed to do, specially where maybe there's going to be some killing done."

Harper paused, wiping at the sweat accumulated on his forehead with the back of a hand. "You ain't never killed a man, have you?" he asked in a tentative voice.

Fortuna loosed the collar of her shirt. The morning had grown hot early, and was staying so despite the light wind that had sprung to life.

"No. Deer, rabbits, quail, and the like. Once I brought down a bear—but never a man."

"Hard to do," Harper said, shrugging. "Makes

a fellow think—and if he holds up to do that, he's liable to get himself killed by the jasper he's figuring to shoot."

"You ever have to shoot a man, Deputy?"

"In the war—yes, but not since I've been toting a badge. Big difference."

Fortuna shifted on her saddle. "Killing is killing, same as dead is dead. I can't see that there's much difference."

"When you put it that way maybe there ain't. Only thing, in war you mostly don't see the man you're shooting at, leastwise not up close. He's just a somebody off somewhere shooting at you. It ain't personal, I reckon you could say."

Fortuna put her eyes on the trail ahead once more, tired of the conversation. She had talked and thought enough about death in the last few hours, and would as soon set her mind on something else. There was no avoiding, of course, the knowledge that such would become a part of her life in the days to come, and she was willing to accept the fact; but there was no need to dwell on it. When the moment came to face it, face it she would, and as Frank often said—let the devil claim the slow gun.

Reaching up, she pulled her hat tighter about her head. The wind was becoming stronger, and it began to look as if they were in for a hard blow. Harper said something, but she paid no heed, wishing as she did that she'd made a stronger stand against bringing him along. Saul was a man inclined to talk—a jaw wagger she'd heard him called; it was a trait she was not accustomed to and had little patience with. But to keep the town fathers happy, and obtain their approval, she had set her dislikes aside. She only hoped that Harper would not prove too much of a hindrance.

But Saul Harper had an endless store of topics to discuss, most of which he pursued to great lengths that first night in camp, and on the following day when they resumed the trail. Fortuna had quickly learned to close not only her ears, but her consciousness as well, merely nodding or shaking her head at intervals as they pressed steadily northward.

The wind had failed to rise to any proportion that first day, but late that next morning it began to make its force noticeable, and by the time Fortuna and Harper reached Haystack Canyon— little more than a deep wash between two low-lying, loaf-shaped hills—it had turned into a fierce, cutting blow.

"I reckon one thing's sure settled," Harper stated when late in the afternoon they rode down into the wash. "There ain't going to be no trail left for to follow. This here wind will've wiped it out for dang sure."

Fortuna nodded. It was a disappointment, but she would not let Saul Harper see it.

"Expect you're right—but it changes nothing. We'll camp for the night, and head out in the morning early."

The deputy rubbed at his jaw. "What way?"

"East. Luke said they rode off in that direction. Like as not there's a town over there somewhere— and that'll be what Red and the others headed for."

CHAPTER 3

Saul Harper looked across the campfire at Fortuna West and sighed. With the flames flickering upon her smooth features, highlighting her cheekbones and accenting her shadowed eyes, she was one hell of a good looker, he thought.

But then he'd always felt that way about her. It was the one thing that had kept him hanging around Frank West's office in Whitehill doing the piddling little odd jobs like serving papers, and looking for lost kids, and sometimes serving as jailer.

If it hadn't been for Fortuna working there now and then also, he'd never have put up with the treatment the marshal and the other deputies accorded him—the same attitude they reserved for saloon swampers, stable hands, and the like. But just being there, seeing her close by, smelling the good, tantalizing woman smell of her, hearing her voice, and watching the parts of her body move and stir gracefully when she walked across the floor, made up for all of the insults and slights he had to endure.

Now he was going to be with Fortuna day and night for maybe weeks to come, which was something to really look forward to. And there'd be nobody to interfere, to get in the way, and prevent his saying a lot of the things that he had in his mind.

Saul reveled in the anticipation, had a wild hope that they just might go on together indefinitely riding across the land hunting for Red Pearson and his sidekicks, and never finding them! He'd like nothing better! And it just might even end up with Fortuna marrying him!

"I sure am sorry the wind's gone and messed up the trail Pearson and them left," Harper said, anxious to get a conversation started. "Going to make it mighty tough to track them down."

Fortuna, staring vacantly into the fire, drew the blanket she had thrown about her shoulders a bit closer. As soon as the sun had gone down it had begun to grow colder.

"Just have to try and figure where they'll most likely go—"

"Same as if we were them."

"I've been trying to remember that map hanging in Frank's office," Fortuna said, frowning. "There's a town, I think, due east of here in Texas. Not certain what it was called—something about a gun. My guess is that's where they headed for."

Frank's office! Saul thought, hearing little of what Fortuna said. *Not any more!* It just could be that—with West and Coleman both dead, Zeke

Tyler turned outlaw, and on the run—he could wind up being the next town marshal. By all rights he should be—he was the only deputy left, and therefore the next in line. Now, wouldn't that be something if things worked out where he had not only the job of old high and mighty Frank West, but his woman, too? That would start old Frank to spinning in his grave like an Independence Day pinwheel!

It occurred to Saul in the succeeding moment that Fortuna could decide she wanted to hang on to the job, be Whitehill's lawman. Almost immediately he brushed that possibility aside. Jake Dietrich and the rest of the town council wouldn't go for it. Hell, they wouldn't have agreed to her going after Pearson and his bunch if he hadn't said he'd go with her!

"What if they ain't in this here town—whatever its name is?" Harper asked, supping at his coffee.

Coyotes were noisily lamenting their lot from the low hills to the west, directing their complaints to a moon riding high overhead in an empty sky. Fortuna listened for a time and then shrugged.

"I'll keep on hunting them—and I'll keep at it until I find them," she said, her voice low and determined. "But it won't be hard. Somebody will have seen them—four hard-looking men—one riding a paint horse."

"Say, that's right!" Harper exclaimed, brightening. "That was a paint horse the marshal rented for Pearson to ride. That'll help us aplenty."

"Folks won't forget seeing Pearson either—that scraggly red beard and mustache, and all that red hair in need of cutting."

"Can about say the same for Tom Benjamin. He's got a knife scar on his neck. And Tyler—he's so skinny he has to put rocks in his pockets so's he can cross the street if the wind's blowing hard."

"I don't recall Benjamin or the other one, Ike Stringer, too well. I saw them out in front of the jail one day, just hanging around, trying to make out like they weren't watching the place. Frank pointed them out, said they were friends of Red Pearson."

"Well, Stringer's the real bad one. Fast gun, I was told. We'll sure have to watch out for him. Were they in on that stagecoach robbery with Red?"

"Frank wasn't sure. He was hoping to turn up something that would tie them in to it, but last I heard—just before he started for Santa Fe with Pearson and the gold—he hadn't."

"If you ask me I'd say they was in on it! It was just they got lucky and ducked out in time while Red got himself caught holding the bag." Saul grinned at his own words. "Got nabbed holding a bag filled with twenty thousand dollars in gold, you might say."

"That's a bit of good luck for us, too," Fortuna said, missing the bit of weak humor. "The gold was all in new coins—just minted, in fact. Anybody spending one will be a man we're looking for. That'll hold true for a while. Another reason why we need to move fast."

"Oh, I expect there's plenty more new double eagles being passed around," Harper said arbitrarily.

"Not likely," Fortuna replied coolly, reaching for a handful of branches to throw onto the fire. "The government only releases new gold to the banks now and then. There probably won't be another shipment into this area for months."

"But don't you reckon some jasper just riding into these parts could have a couple of brand-new double eagles in his poke that he got when he was somewheres else?"

Fortuna swore irritably under her breath. "Of course that's possible," she replied. "But I'm banking on the odds all being against it."

Harper thought for a moment, and then tossed the remaining drops of coffee in his cup aside. He had rubbed Fortuna the wrong way, arguing a bit with her, and he sure didn't want to do that.

"Expect you're right," he said, and then added, "I'm mighty glad you figure to go on hunting that bunch if we don't find them in that Texas town—"

"We'll catch up with them somewhere," Fortuna said, and drawing the wool cover about her body, stretched out by the fire. "Best you get some sleep. Want to get started by first light."

"Just what I was thinking," the deputy agreed, and pulling his blanket closer, started to lie back.

He paused. "Now, you sure you're going to be warm enough, Fortuna?"

Saul's mouth cracked into a surprised grin. He had called her by her given name—the first and only time he ever had! It had just slipped out, sort of naturally, and it pleased him to see how easily it had happened. He guessed being together like they were was starting to change things between them for the better.

"I'll be fine, Deputy," Fortuna murmured. "I'm no stranger to sleeping out in the open like this."

Every man has his own private dream—his one great hope. Some seek fame, some great riches, others attainment of high stature, or no more than a simple, quiet life. And there are those who want only one day to have the woman for whom they have long hungered. In those hushed moments beneath a star-cluttered sky Saul Harper, one of the latter, felt he was near to realizing his dream.

"Thought maybe—it being a mite cold—we could sort of share the blankets—keep warm that way."

Fortuna West's response was so low he could scarcely hear it. "No need, Deputy. If you get cold there're a couple more blankets in the pack. Help yourself."

Saul was motionless for a time, and then lay back. He'd been a damn fool to come right out like that! Hell, Frank West was barely in his grave! He realized now he should have waited a few days before he made a suggestion like that, let the memory of her husband sort of fade from her mind, and the loneliness set in. Her answer would be different then, he was willing to bet.

They rode east shortly after first light. The day promised to be clear and hot, and Fortuna was grateful there was no promise of wind in the air—not that she expected to find any traces of the outlaws' passage. The blow that previous day had ended all hopes for such; it was simply that traveling would be more pleasant without it.

She cast a side-glance at Harper. The deputy had been unusually quiet ever since they had awakened, seemingly having something on his mind. Fortuna decided not to make any inquiries as to the reason for his silence; it was much nicer without his continual chatter.

The country looked dry, she noted, following the habit of all who lived in an arid land who make such appraisals whether it is of any importance to them or not. Spring rain had apparently been light, just as it had been that summer—but of course the time for the mid-year heavy showers was still a month or so away. The range would green up then.

A covey of quail burst suddenly from the brush nearby, startling the horses, and sending them shying to one side. Harper watched the stubby-winged birds go sailing noisily off toward a thick stand of apache plume, and disappear into its feathery depths.

"Had my scatter-gun I could've got us a few of them for supper," he said, breaking his silence. "They'd taste mighty good."

Fortuna nodded absently. Her glance was on a dozen or so vultures in the sky beyond where the quail had plummeted from sight. As she followed them with her eyes several dropped lower, and were soon beyond view. Something was down, and the big, broad-winged scavengers were having their way with it. Saul focused on the objects of her attention.

"Probably a steer," he said. "Could tell if it wasn't for that ridge."

Fortuna was not so certain. "I don't think there're any ranches nearby. No water anywhere for the stock."

"Could be a deer that's wandered down from the hills, or maybe even a coyote that's gone and died off for some reason. Could be a rabbit, too."

"It'll have to be a fairly large animal to draw so many buzzards—"

"Yeh, guess you're right. Won't be nothing little like a cottontail or a jackrabbit."

They rode on, drawing steadily abreast of the birds, some rising to rejoin those circling above, others remaining behind the weedy berm that slanted off the trail.

"Say—ain't that a horse standing off there by them cedars?"

At Saul Harper's sudden question Fortuna brought her attention to bear on the point indicated by the deputy's leveled finger.

"It is. Looks like it might be a man those buzzards are after," Fortuna replied.

Immediately she swung the sorrel gelding she

was riding off the roadway, and started cross-country for the solitary horse. Harper, hampered somewhat by the pack animal, was a bit slow to follow, but catch up he did. A low whistle of surprise escaped his lips as they drew near.

"Hell—that there's Zeke Tyler's horse!"

"Zeke—Zeke Tyler?" Fortuna echoed, frowning, and raked the sorrel with her spurs.

As the gelding broke into a quick gallop Fortuna drew her pistol. Reaching the sandy ridge beyond which the horse stood she pulled to a halt. The vultures were gathered about a dark object lying on the floor of a narrow wash. Raising her weapon Fortuna fired a shot. At the sharp report the birds instantly leaped into the air with a confusion of flapping wings. It was a man. She could make out a figure now. Once more using her rowels in the sorrel, Fortuna hurried in closer.

A wave of nausea swept her when she gained the ravine—and there had been no need for haste. The vultures, and probably several coyotes and wolves, had already ravaged the body, leaving scarcely anything but cloth and bones. Fortuna turned as Harper pulled in beside her.

"It's Tyler all right. Pearson and the others evidently killed him—and left him laying there for the buzzards to take care of."

CHAPTER 4

"Been shot in the back of the head," Saul Harper reported, now off his horse, and looking more closely at the mutilated corpse. The stench was sickening, and Fortuna was compelled to hold a handkerchief to her face. Harper, however, seemed unaffected. "Somebody sure got him from behind. I'm wondering who, and why."

Fortuna's shoulders stirred indifferently. She had no sympathy for the man, a trusted deputy and friend of her husband's, who had been a party to his murder, and was in no way interested in delving into the reasons why Tyler had been killed.

Nevertheless, burying the remains was only decent, regardless of how she felt, and motioning for Saul to assist, caved in the sides of the wash over the body, and then dragging up what brush was available, piled it on top to complete the grave. Turning away she glanced at Tyler's abandoned horse.

"Can't leave him standing there," she said, taking her canteen and crossing to where the animal waited. "Wolves will pull him down sure."

Harper, watching her grasp the horse's lower jaw, force it open, and pour a small quantity of water into the animal's mouth, frowned. "Can't hardly take him along—"

"What we'll have to do. Maybe'll slow us down a bit but we can leave him at the first town we come to," Fortuna said, and taking up the reins of the gray, led him to where the other mounts were waiting.

"I'm still wondering who shot Zeke," Harper said when they were once again under way.

"My guess it was Pearson—"

"Pearson? Luke Coleman said Zeke had throwed in with them. Now why—"

"Probably just used Zeke. It was his job to bring Frank to the place where the ambush was to take place. After he did that they were through with him."

Harper mulled that about for a long minute. "Yep, I'll bet that's just how it was. Red and the others told him they'd split the gold with him to get him to do it. Never aimed to at all. Soon as it was done they put a bullet in his head instead."

Fortuna was only half listening, but she nodded. Only three outlaws were left now: Pearson, Benjamin, and Ike Stringer. That improved the odds considerably. Too, there was no doubt now that she was on the right trail. Finding Tyler's ravaged body nearby made that apparent.

"Zeke was sort of loco," she heard Harper say.

"I don't mean crazy-crazy, but funny crazy. Showed in the way he looked at things."

Fortuna glanced ahead, her eyes drifting slowly over the vast, empty land. The hills were barely rises, and there was little vegetation to be seen— snakeweed, sharptipped bayonet yucca, cholla cactus, an occasional thinleafed mesquite.

"He always claimed that being decent and honest wasn't for poor folks, that they couldn't afford to be that way. And anyway, he'd say, every man, rich or poor, has his hand out for something."

"I didn't realize Tyler felt that way about things," Fortuna said, Harper finally catching her full attention. "I don't think Frank did either."

"He hated the marshal," Harper observed blandly. "Sure don't like saying that, but it's the truth. And he didn't like being a part-time deputy either. Told me once if he could ever find himself another job, he'd quit mighty quick and take it.

"Was tired of being a nothing, a nobody, he said, and he was looking for the chance someday to grab a bag of money, no matter who it belonged to, and run for it."

"I guess that explains why he threw in with Pearson and the others. He thought he'd get a share of the twenty thousand dollars."

"But what he got was a bullet in the head," the deputy said with a wry grin. "I'll bet he didn't figure that'd happen!"

Man lays down with the pigs, he's going to get mud on him, Fortuna recalled Frank saying on a

similar incident. It applied to Zeke Tyler. He'd
chosen to ignore his oath to uphold the law, had
joined with outlaws, and committed murder. He
couldn't expect the company he'd picked to be
men of honor since they were no different from
him, and equally untrustworthy.

They rode on, now following a more definite
trail that cut in from the north, and bore due
southeast. Around noon they halted in an arroyo
where a cluster of mesquite trees offered a smat-
tering of filigree shade, ate a bit of lunch, and
after relieving the horses' thirst with water from
their canteens, resumed the journey.

"That dang town must be clean over on the
other side of Texas," Harper complained when,
hours later, there were still no signs of a
settlement.

Fortuna was beginning to entertain similar
thoughts. But it wouldn't matter; the hunt would
go on. The cold, angry determination to find, and
bring to account, the men who had murdered her
husband had not decreased; indeed, with the passing of time it had strengthened. She was as resolute now, after two days and a night on the trail,
to track down Red Pearson and his friends, as
she was at the start, though it might take until
doomsday.

And then late in the afternoon with the hot
sun hammering at their backs, they saw smoke
twisting up into empty blue sky, and a time later
came to a pair of crude signs erected at a fork in
the trail. One pointed off to the left—the north—

and bore the inscription: HANGING TREE RANCH. The other, directed toward the east, stated simply: GUNFIRE.

"That'll be the town we're looking for," Harper said.

Fortuna, tension beginning to build within her, nodded, and they continued on. A little more than an hour later they reached the settlement—a helter-skelter collection of dilapidated, decaying buildings and huts scattered about several stock pens built along the rusting rails of a railroad spur—one evidently long abandoned.

"It sure ain't much," Saul Harper observed sourly as they halted at the end of a narrow, dusty street. "Looks like everybody's done moved out."

Gunfire did appear to be mostly deserted, Fortuna admitted with lowering spirits. Red Pearson was not likely to be found there; he'd seek a larger town, one where the opportunities for spending his newly acquired riches would be more inviting. But she was equally certain that the outlaw and his two friends had been there; the need that lay before her now was to find out which direction the killers had taken when they rode on.

"We staying the night here?" Harper asked.

Fortuna swept the structures along the empty street with her glance. The Texas Rose Saloon, Hobbs General Store, and a livery stable that displayed no name appeared to be the only going concerns in the settlement.

"I doubt there'll be any reason to," she replied. "Take the horses over to that livery stable, and water and feed them. I'll meet you in the saloon. I want to find out if anybody saw Pearson, and knows which trail he took when he left here."

"Could still be around," the deputy said. "Bunch of horses back there behind the saloon."

"A chance, but I figure they're gone. Pearson wouldn't spend any time in a place like this, but I'll have a look at the hitch rack for a pinto before I go in."

Harper rubbed at his jaw and frowned. "You think it's smart you going in there alone?"

Fortuna's mouth tightened. This would be the first test, her initial attempt at being a lawman, and the pressure of that realization was suddenly bearing down upon her. Had she been a woman of lesser will, she would have in all probability panicked at the prospect of entering a saloon filled with disapproving men, outlaws, hardcase trail riders, and saddle tramps, but the sullen rage glowing within her overcame all thoughts of personal fear.

"I'll be all right, Deputy. Can tell the livery stable owner that we found Tyler's horse—no need explaining more than that," Fortuna said, and came down off her sorrel.

Harper, dismounting, took the gelding's reins. "Now, you best watch yourself in there. Place like that's plenty tough . . . I'll be along soon as I can."

Fortuna made no reply. She was engrossed in

her own thoughts—of what she would say when she was inside the Texas Rose—of what she would do if matters didn't go her way. After a few moments she shrugged the problem aside; there was no easy answer to either question. She'd simply face up to the issue, and react according to her instincts.

Drawing abreast the hitch rack where a number of horses were standing in slope-hipped weariness, Fortuna gave them quick scrutiny. There was no pinto among them, which was what she expected, and continuing on, headed for the entrance to the Texas Rose—a single door opened wide in deference to the heat.

Stepping inside she collided instantly with a wall of smoke, sound, and the odors of whiskey and sweat. There were a dozen or more patrons present—cowhands, trail riders, hard cases, and the like, just as she had expected. A lone bartender stood behind the counter, and two frowzy women were holding court at a back table.

Hanging tight to her nerves, aware that all eyes were suddenly upon her, Fortuna crossed to the bar, and took a place in the line of men bellied up to it. The barkeeper, dressed no differently from the patrons he served, glanced inquiringly at her.

"Yes'm?"

"I'm looking for three men," Fortuna said. "Names probably won't mean anything to you, but one is a redhead called Pearson. Others are Benjamin and Stringer."

She paused. Absolute stillness had closed in over the saloon. The man immediately to her right came half about, a squat, beefy individual with a ragged, dirty beard and mustache, and eyes reddened from prolonged drinking. He considered her warily.

The bartender shook his head. "Lady, I make it a habit to never pass on any information," he began, and stopped short when Fortuna drew back the front of her doeskin jacket to reveal the star pinned to her shirt.

"Maybe this'll change your habits," she said. "I'm the law. I want these men for murder—and I know they came here. Now—"

"What do you know—a lady lawman!" the beefy man beside her shouted. Reaching out quickly he jerked the hat off her head. As hair spilled down about her shoulders, he added: "And a red-headed one at that!"

Fortuna, confused, off balance, drew back from the drunk. At that moment Saul Harper came through the doorway. He saw in a glance what was taking place, and rushed in between Fortuna and the man.

"Back off!" the deputy shouted. "Or—"

"Or what?" the husky drunk demanded, and drove a rock hard fist into Harper's jaw.

The deputy staggered, fell into a chair, and then against a table that overturned and spilled him sprawling onto the floor. Saul yelled, clutched at his left leg, twisted beneath him.

The drunk grinned, turned back to Fortuna.

Pressed against the bar, she was trapped, motionless, seemingly paralyzed by the swift turn of events, and unable to move.

"Now, let's just see what else this here lady lawman's got to show us besides that tin star!" the drunk said, and reached for the front of Fortuna's shirt.

CHAPTER 5

Cheers filled the saloon. A voice shouted: "Go to it, Jubal!"

Fortuna West, sudden ungovernable fear gripping her as eager, liquor-flushed, grinning faces pressed in about her, recoiled further. She raised her hands to ward off Jubal's clawing fingers, glancing appealingly at Saul Harper.

She would get no help from the deputy. He lay amid the wreckage of a chair, the overturned table resting on his shoulder. Pain distorted his features as he endeavored to disentangle his injured leg, unquestionably broken, and sit up.

"A danged lady lawman!" Jubal boomed in a loud voice. "You reckon she's the same as any other female?"

"Find out, Jubal!" someone encouraged. "Find out!"

"Just what I'll do," the heavy-set rider shouted, and again reached for Fortuna.

Abruptly a hand fell on Jubal's shoulder, and spun him roughly about. A tall, vaguely familiar, hard-faced man crowded in close. Moving swiftly, he sent the drunk stumbling and cursing back into the circle of onlookers.

"Best you forget it," the tall man said coolly.

Again shouts echoed through the Texas Rose—this time of disapproval.

"You forget it, Luttrel!" a voice in the crowd countered. "This ain't none of your put-in!"

Luttrel folded his arms across his chest. "I'm making it mine."

Fortuna West, recovering her hat from the bar where the drunk had tossed it, placed it on her head, and quickly tucked her hair into place. She was stunned, shocked. Matters had not gone at all the way she had expected; the fact she was a woman had completely overridden the authority of the star she wore.

"Get out of here, Deputy, if that's what you are," Luttrel said in a low, harsh tone. "Too many of them for me if they take it in mind to go ahead with Jubal's little peeling party."

Luttrel had thick, dark brows, small agatelike eyes that glittered in the lamplight, and a hard line for a mouth. Dressed in usual range fashion—leather vest, shield shirt, brown cord pants, and stovepipe boots, he wore a high-crowned, uncreased gray hat with a snakeskin band.

"Now," he muttered, urgency in his tone.

Fortuna could scarcely hear him above the clamoring of the unruly crowd, but his meaning came through. She turned and crossed to Saul Harper. One of the bystanders was assisting him to rise.

"His leg's busted, ma'am," he said, and then

added softly: "Them fellows you was asking for—they rode south."

Fortuna nodded slightly, and hung Harper's arm about her neck. Supporting the deputy as best she could, the woman started for the doorway, giving rise to a fresh burst of yells. Fortuna did not pause to look back. There was no quick rap of boot heels, and from that guessed she was not being followed. The man they called Luttrel was apparently still having his way.

The fresh air brought a rush of full consciousness to Saul Harper when they reached the saloon's landing, and moved down into the street.

"Where we going?" he asked, hobbling along as best he could. "I'm hurting something fierce."

"To the livery stable," Fortuna replied. As large and strong as she was Harper's leaning upon her was making itself felt. "We'll see if we can get some help there."

Inwardly she was still trembling from the incident in the saloon, and now anger, mixed with chagrin and shame at her failure, was claiming her. What she had thought would be no more than a matter of procedure, one of merely asking questions—the answers to which would come immediately upon the displaying of her star—had turned into a fiasco, a joke. If it hadn't been for the tall man with the snakeskin hatband, Luttrel—Fortuna's lips tightened at the thought—she would have been in for a bad time of it.

The livery stable was just ahead. Reaching the opening in its forward wall Fortuna now glanced toward the saloon; there was no sign of anyone behind them. Continuing, with Saul Harper sagging against her, she stepped inside.

"There a hostler or somebody here?" she asked the deputy.

He nodded, and shouted a name. Moments later an elderly man came from a room at the end of the stable's runway. When he saw Harper, he halted.

"You after them dang horses a-ready? They ain't hardly got to eating. . . . There something wrong with your leg?"

"Busted," Saul replied. "Got in a fracas over at the saloon."

The hostler clucked sympathetically. "Was with that damn Jubal Boone and his bunch, I'll bet." He transferred his attention to Fortuna, considered her thoughtfully in the weak light from a nearby lantern. Then, "Howdy, ma'am. . . . Reckon you ain't wanting them horses after all—seeing how you ain't about to do no riding," he added, again facing Harper.

"No," Fortuna said, "what we want to know is where the deputy can get his leg fixed. Anybody around here do that?"

The hostler bobbed. "I reckon so. Old Doc Mitchell's still doing doctoring. He ain't much but I expect he can take care of a busted leg."

"Where'll we find him?"

"Down the street a piece—on the left," the hostler said, pointing. "Can see the sign over his door if you look right smart. What about them horses?"

"Let them eat—we'll be back later," Fortuna said, and still supporting Harper returned to the street, cut left, and began to look for the residence or office of the town's physician.

"Guess this means we'll be heading back for Whitehill," the deputy said as they made their way slowly along through the closing darkness. "You've done learned a woman can't be no deputy, and with me all stove in with a busted leg to where I can't side you, you just ain't got no other choice."

Fortuna nodded absently, but her mind was elsewhere, coolly sorting out what had taken place. It had been her fault that matters had gotten out of control. She recalled now Frank once telling her that a lawman had to always maintain the upper hand, and never show uncertainty or indecision; *let them know, by God, you're calling the shots, and if it takes a rap across the skull with your six-shooter to prove it—don't hold back!*

That was where she had gone wrong, Fortuna scolded herself. The instant that drunk—Jubal—had jerked off her hat she should have buffaloed him with her gun, and then made it clear to the rest of the men in the saloon that the next one of them who thought she was a joke, and got out of line with her, would wind up with a bullet hole in his hide.

"Here's the place," she heard Harper say.

Turning to the sagging, single-storied building

she saw the sign over the doorway that indicated the physician's residence, and entered the yard. Deep inside the house she could see a light, and was relieved to find Mitchell at home. Allowing Harper to rest against the wall, she knocked on the door. A voice shouted for her to enter.

Twisting the metal knob, Fortuna helped the deputy into a stuffy, heat-laden room, paused briefly, and continued on to the rear of the house where a lamp was burning. It was the kitchen. They had caught Mitchell at his evening meal. He sat alone at a bare table, a bowl of stew before him, a cup and a pot of coffee close by.

At the appearance of Fortuna West and Harper, he laid down the spoon he was holding, and stared at them frowningly.

"Thought you were Pete," he said, and settled his eyes on the deputy's injured member. "Broke yur leg, eh? Ain't seen one of them in quite a spell—not since they quit shipping cattle out of here. About all I get any more is a bullet hole, or maybe some beat-up drunk."

"Like for you to take care of it for him," Fortuna said.

Mitchell took a sip of coffee. "Sure. All it'll take is a couple of dollars."

Fortuna reached into a side pocket for the specified amount, but Harper shook his head. Resting himself against the table, he dug into his own pocket for the money.

"I reckon I can pay my own way," he said, and dropping a pair of silver coins in front of the doctor, turned to Fortuna. "I heard what that bird said about Pearson and them heading south. Now, we ain't chasing after them—not with me all crippled up. You can mighty quick see what we'd be up against."

"You can't ride, that's for certain," she agreed.

"And you can't take out after them by yourself—"

Why not? Fortuna considered the thought. It wouldn't be easy, and far from safe; her experience in the Texas Rose told her that. But such encounters didn't have to turn out as that one had; it wouldn't have if she'd handled it right. And she now had definite information as to which trail the outlaws, men she'd vowed to overtake and bring to justice for murdering her husband, had taken. It would be foolish to not press that advantage.

"You're right, Deputy," Fortuna said, coming to a decision. "You're in no shape to go on—and you wouldn't be any use to me if you were along. Thing I want you to do is lay around here for a spell, and then when you can set a saddle, head back to Whitehill."

A frown clouded Saul Harper's leathery features. "You mean you're going after that bunch?"

"I'll have to—"

"Can't no woman do that! Hell, you seen that star didn't mean nothing when—"

"It will the next time," Fortuna cut in. "When you get back to town tell the council—or anybody else that's interested—that everything's all right.

. . . You got enough money for grub and such?" she added, turning to leave.

"Sure, sure," Harper grumbled. "Now, you hadn't ought to be doing this—it's downright foolish! It'll serve you right if something bad happens—and I ain't going to let them blame me!"

"Nobody will," Fortuna said, and hurried on.

CHAPTER 6

Fortuna doubled back up the dusty street to the livery stable. Darkness was almost complete now, and she supposed it would be smart to spend the night in Gunfire, but as there was no hotel doing business, she reckoned she would be as well off in a camp along the trail. Besides, the sooner she rode on after Red Pearson and his friends, the better.

The hostler was nowhere to be found when she reached the livery barn, and now anxious to be on her way, she located the sorrel, saddled and bridled him, and made ready the pack horse. That done, she filled her canteen with fresh water from the pump at the trough, mounted up, and rode out trailing the pack horse behind at the end of a short lead rope. To pay for the feeding of the two animals, Fortuna left a silver dollar on the stable owner's desk.

As she entered the street the thought to drop back and cross behind the Texas Rose occurred to her. In so doing she would avoid being seen by anyone who happened to be loitering about the saloon's entrance. With a shrug she dismissed precaution; she was a lawman, and it was high time she started acting and thinking like one. Raking the sorrel lightly with her spurs she struck boldly down the center of the street for the trail south.

Never again would she let any man—outlaw or otherwise—intimidate her as the drunk, Jubal, had. She supposed she should feel grateful to him; she had learned a very valuable lesson in the Texas Rose, one at low cost to herself—and she certainly intended to benefit from it. A lawman had to present a positive front, never betraying uncertainty or hesitation, regardless of the odds faced; and regardless of the odds, not allow herself to be bluffed out of what she felt had to be done.

She came abreast the Texas Rose. Lamplight was now spilling through the open doorway into the street, and turning her head, Fortuna threw her glance into the saloon. Two men stood just within its entrance, bearded features facing her. Beyond in the smoky depths of the building the line of patrons bellied up to the bar was visible, and past them in the bluish haze were the indefinite outlines of other customers. The pair in the doorway showed no interest in her departure, she noted, but merely watched as she rode on by into the growing night.

She thought she caught a glimpse of the tall man who had stepped in between her and Jubal, and turned the drunk aside, but the interior of the saloon was so murky that she couldn't be sure. Actually, the meeting with him had been so brief that she'd not gotten a very good look at him, but there was something familiar about the man—Luttrel, she recalled someone calling him—familiar both in looks and in name.

Fortuna reached the edge of the settlement with the rider's name rolling about in her mind, and guided the sorrel onto the trail that angled off into the southwest. She'd ride on for another hour or two since the horses had both been fed, watered, and rested for a bit, and then make camp. Although it had not been possible to find out when Pearson and his friends had left Gunfire, she felt certain the outlaws were not too far ahead of her.

Outlaws—Luttrel! Remembrance hit Fortuna in a sudden gust. The tall man's name was Ben Luttrel. She had seen his picture on one of the wanted posters in Frank West's desk—an outlaw wanted for murder!

Fortuna smiled wryly, the thought of a killer coming to her aid striking her as a strange twist. She couldn't recall the details of the charge against Luttrel, had not in fact read beyond the name, and the statement that he was a hired gun wanted for murder.

Luttrel was the type, Fortuna supposed, if you could say there was a specific type; dark-faced, cool, withdrawn manner, a fearless, even deadly, way about him that commanded immediate respect. He had certainly backed Jubal off, and settled down the crowd—at least long enough for her, in company with Saul Harper, to get out of the saloon. What had taken place after that she had no way of knowing, but there had been no gunshots, and that apparently indicated Jubal and his noisy followers had thought better of challenging Luttrel.

She had failed to acknowledge the favor he had extended her, Fortuna realized, and had in no way thanked him. She wished now she'd taken a moment to do so—wanting in no way to be obligated to an outlaw—but her need to get out of the Texas Rose quickly had been matched equally by his urging her to leave. She doubted she'd ever see Ben Luttrel again, but if such came to pass, she would make a point of expressing her appreciation.

Fortuna made camp in a cluster of small trees a time later. She wasn't hungry, and bypassed building a fire to prepare a meal. Later she slept only fitfully, her mind still on the incident in the Gunfire saloon where she had literally turned and run when afforded the chance. The remembrance of having done so was like a dark, undissolving shadow lodged in her thoughts.

She rose early, prepared a hasty breakfast of fried meat, warmed bread, and coffee, and was back on the trail shortly after first light. With the coming of morning the deep, stark loneliness she felt at Frank West's absence each night since his death had retreated again into her conscious-

ness, and the problems the new day was certain
to bring claimed her attention.

She was crossing a broad land somewhere near
the Staked Plains, Fortuna guessed. It was unfamiliar country, a vast, magnificent area sobering
in its majestic emptiness. Noon came, and again
not hungry, she halted only to rest the horses
after which she was once more in the saddle, and
pressed on persistently. The feeling that she was
drawing close to Red Pearson and the other men
was strong within her, and she was grimly preparing herself for the confrontation.

Around mid-afternoon she saw a town on the
crown of a fairly high rise well ahead. There was
no smoke, and it occurred to her that it was
likely another of those settlements that sprang
into life for reasons of being on a cattle trail, and
offering a stopover for watering stock, or perhaps
a shipping point as Gunfire had apparently been.
Then, when their excuse for existence ended they
fell into disuse, and eventually were abandoned
completely. Gunfire was on its way to that finale
just as this place probably was.

But the settlement on the rise—Mulehead, according to a sign—was far from that state, Fortuna
saw as she drew to a halt at its edge. There
appeared to be several stores and at least three
saloons doing business. She noted two women
crossing the street as if shopping, and horses
stood at different hitch racks along the way.

This most certainly was a likely place to find
Red Pearson, Benjamin, and Ike Stringer—a town

large enough for them to spend and enjoy some of the stolen gold. Touching the sorrel with her rowels, Fortuna turned into the settlement, and moved toward its center.

Red Pearson took the stogie from between his teeth, exhaled a cloud of smoke from his lungs, accepted the bottle of whiskey Ike Stringer offered him, and helped himself to a satisfying drink. Smacking his lips, he passed the liquor on to Tom Benjamin.

"A man sure can't appreciate being free and on his own until he's been locked up for a spell," Pearson said, tossing a handful of dry branches onto the campfire. They had halted in a somewhat shallow arroyo for lack of a better place.

"Same as he don't appreciate good liquor until he's had to drink rotgut all his life," Stringer added.

"For damn sure! Being rich is a mighty fine feeling," Pearson declared, again puffing at the stogie.

"Richer'n we figured makes it even better," Benjamin said, returning the bottle of whiskey to Stringer. "Was real smart thinking, Red—you flim-flamming that deputy into fixing things up for us so's we'd have a cinch with them lawmen—"

"And then putting a bullet in his head when he started bellyaching for his share," Stringer finished. "Made it a three-way split instead of four."

"I had it all worked out a'fore time," Pearson said, basking in the glow of compliments. "That's what a man has to do—get everything all set, then make his move. That damned marshal and his deputy never knew what hit them when you boys opened up with your sixshooters."

"They sure was surprised, all right," Stringer agreed. "And best thing about it is there probably ain't nobody wise yet as to what happened. Be another day or two before they're supposed to show up in Santa Fe with you and the gold. Then it'll take a couple more days, maybe longer, for the U.S. marshal up there to start wondering why you ain't showed up, and start looking."

"Got to hand it to you, Red—that's for certain," Benjamin said, glancing toward the horses barely visible in the nearby brush. "When we splitting up the gold? My pockets are running dry—specially after buying that whiskey back there in that town—Mulehead, or whatever they called it."

"Ain't no big hurry," Pearson drawled with a wave of his hand. "It's safe right there in them saddlebags on my pinto."

"Been sort of worrying about that horse," Stringer said. "Kind of like riding a sign board. Anybody on the watch for us could spot us a mile off. I'm thinking you'd be smart to trade him off for something that folks won't notice so quick— seeing as how by now everybody knows that one of us is riding a paint."

Pearson shrugged. "Like you said we probably ain't even been missed yet so there won't be nobody on the lookout for us. Anyway, I reckon pintos are sort of common around here—and he's a good riding horse with plenty of bottom."

"Always heard them light-haired animals wasn't much. Was told they got a sore back real easy."

"Heard the same tale," Pearson said, "but it ain't exactly for true. My pa was a great one for horses, and he always claimed a paint was all right long as you didn't get one with a white back. Said white, or any light color made for a tender hide. Get one where black or dark brown color is under the saddle, and a man'll never have no trouble, so he told me."

"Wasn't thinking so much about him giving out on you as I was about folks remembering us when the law starts hunting for our trail."

"And you can bet there'll be aplenty of them doing that!" Benjamin stated, reaching for the whiskey. "Killing two lawmen—three if you're counting that Tyler—is sure going to set them on their ear! Every badge toter from hell to hallelujah will be looking for us."

"Don't fret none about that," Pearson said indifferently. "By the time they figure out what happened, and start searching, we'll be across the border in Mexico."

"I'm sure hoping so," Benjamin said. "Ike and me ain't never been down this far before. You for sure we're headed right—following the right trail, I mean?"

"Hell, it don't make no difference what trail a man follows if he wants to go to Mexico—he just has to keep riding south."

"You been there before—Mexico?"

Pearson took the lifeless butt of the stogie from between his teeth and flipped it into the dwindling fire.

"No, new country to me same as it is to you. But like I said, a man can't go wrong long as he keeps pointing south. Sooner or later he's going to come to the border."

Tom Benjamin swore softly, and lay back. "Well, that can't come too soon for me," he muttered as he closed his eyes. "What say we get some shut-eye so's we can head out early?"

CHAPTER 7

The Star ... the Cimarron ... Happy Jim's.
Those were the saloons of Mulehead, Fortuna
saw. She halted at the first, a low, unplastered
adobe affair, and tying the sorrel and pack horse
at the hitch rack—coolly ignoring the stare turned
to her by a man and a woman emerging from
close by Peabody's General Store—she gripped
her courage and entered the shadow-filled Star.

There were but three men present, and all were
at the bar. Remembering the lesson she'd learned
in Gunfire, Fortuna swept them with a hard,
straight look, pivoted on a heel, and returned to
the street. Pearson and his two partners would
not have patronized a rag-tag, hole-in-the-wall
place like the Star; they would seek out one of
the larger saloons where amusement of every
kind would be available.

That would be Happy Jim's, she decided, giving only a cursory glance at the Cimarron—a
wood and corrugated tin affair of the same caliber as the Star. Happy Jim's was considerably
larger, had a high false front across the upper

portion of which blazed the name and the fact
that whiskey, women, dancing, and gambling could
all be found beneath its slanting roof.

Leaving the horses where they stood at the
Star's rack, Fortuna strode purposefully toward
Happy Jim's. As she drew near, the sound of a
piano and the rhythmic thump of booted feet
keeping time reached her. Again she was conscious of eyes being turned upon her, this time
from two men standing a bit to the left of the
saloon's entrance. She wasn't certain, but it could
be they had caught sight of her star, visible at
times when the front of her fringed jacket flared
open as she walked.

A taut grin pulled at her lips. Let them look—
and wonder—it didn't matter. Her confidence was
complete. She knew how to handle herself, and
knew also how to impress upon those whom she
might face the need for respecting the badge of
authority she was wearing.

Reaching the double door of Happy Jim's, both
opened wide, Fortuna entered. The place was well
patronized—two dozen or more men being in evidence even at that early hour—and provided at
least half that number of gaudily dressed, painted
women for their use. At the moment some were
engaged in dancing, others were sitting at tables,
lounging at the bar, or hanging about the gam-
blers in an area off to one side provided for such.

There was an upper floor, Fortuna saw, dimly
lit by wall lamps, but she could make out a hall-
way running from the balcony at right angles,

and off which several doors apparently turned. These would be rooms where the women could entertain customers.

Striding directly into the wide, noise-filled room with its hovering layers of smoke and smells, Fortuna halted at a point where she had a view of everyone on the lower floor. Coolly ignoring the faces turned to her, she swept the crowd with her glance. Red Pearson was not present. He could be on the upper floor, of course, with one of the girls. Fortuna's lips tightened. If it came down to that, she'd climb the stair, enter the hall, and canvass each room and its occupants. This would create considerable ill feeling, Fortuna knew, but she'd not let that bother her; she was the law, and had the right as well as the obligation to search for the killers she was pursuing.

But first it would not only be wise, it would also save time, to find out from the bartender, or perhaps the women, if Pearson and his friends were there, and if so, just where they were. Coming about, she walked to the bar, pushed in between two men, and nodded briskly to the bartender. It had required considerable nerve and courage to boldly force a place for herself along the counter, and she couldn't ignore the trembling within her; but when it was done and she'd not been challenged, Fortuna not only felt better but was also aware of her courage rising even higher.

"I'm looking for three men," she said in a firm voice, flipping aside the front of her jacket so that the barkeep could see her star. Earlier she had pondered the advisability of concealing her status as a lawman, thinking perhaps the men she questioned might be reluctant to talk. But after mulling it about in her mind she decided against such deception; the star represented authority, and as such it likely more often than not would aid her in getting the answers she sought.

"Three men," she repeated as the bartender's face stilled, and the patrons to either side of her pulled slightly away. "Names were Pearson, Benjamin, and Stringer. First one's red-headed, and was riding a pinto horse. Benjamin's got a knife scar on his neck. Can't tell you much about Stringer other than it's said he's a gunman."

The bartender frowned, brushed at his mustache, and glanced about. Except for the immediate area where Fortuna stood, the saloon had resumed activity, and those within it were paying no mind to what they assumed was a man in a fringed doeskin jacket and flat crowned hat who had entered and was now at the bar getting a drink.

"Yeh, they was here, Deputy," the barkeep said finally in a reluctant tone. "Showed up yesterday, hung around all night, drinking and dancing and messing with the girls. Rode off early this morning."

"Which way?" Fortuna asked, keeping her voice strong and level. She could feel the eyes of nearby men upon her—drilling, curious.

'Now, that ain't something I'd know," the barkeep said. "Talk to the girls. Maybe one of them can help you."

"I seen them," the man beyond the one next to Fortuna at the counter volunteered. "Was when I was coming into town—about daylight."

"Headed what direction?" Fortuna pressed, her words clipped and to the point.

'Why, south. They was following the trail along Sulphur Creek."

Fortuna nodded briskly to her informant, then to the bartender, and close-by patrons who had been witness to the conversation.

"I'm obliged to you," she said, and wheeling, retraced her steps to the doorway and out into the street.

A feeling of relief and pride was coursing through her as she returned to the horses. She had remembered what Frank had said about presenting a hard-nosed, no-nonsense front at such times—and it had worked. She had been accorded the respect a lawman was due—and there'd been no snickering about a woman wearing a star.

Mounting the sorrel, and taking up the lead rope of the gray pack horse, Fortuna, well satisfied with the way things had turned out, rode on down the street, past the Cimarron, Happy Jim's, and the other enterprises at that end of the settlement, and on out onto the trail. Sulphur Creek she found quickly. It was a small stream that apparently cut in from the west and angled south. The trail, well used to judge from its hard-packed condition, closely followed its course.

Red Pearson, Benjamin, and Ike Stringer had been seen early that morning—riding south. That meant they would now be only a day ahead of her, but more satisfaction came with the knowledge that she was still on their heels. She had only to catch up, to overtake them—and she was near enough now to do just that if they dallied again in some town along the way, or took their time in breaking morning camp, and moving on.

And there was no reason as far as they knew to hurry. The outlaws would believe they had left a closed trail behind them, one that nobody would take up for days since they were unaware that Luke Coleman had not died in the ambush, but had lived to tell of Frank West's murder, and put her in the saddle in pursuit of them.

Twisting about, Fortuna threw her glance back to Mulehead. The settlement, perched on its rise, was now darkly outlined by the lowering sun. Smoke was spiraling upward from several pipe chimneys as housewives went about preparing the evening meal for their families, and a short distance beyond the scatter of structures a solitary rider was coming in from the direction of Gunfire.

That turned her thoughts to Saul Harper. Soon he would be starting for Whitehill, carrying with him a report of what had happened in the Texas Rose saloon—and making it clear to everyone that he had done his best to persuade her not to continue alone after Red Pearson and the men with him.

This would stir up plenty of talk in the settlement. There was little doubt of that, Fortuna thought with a wry smile as she rode steadily on at a better-than-average pace. But it didn't matter what anyone said; eventually she would come upon the killers of her husband and take them back to hang for what they had done.

Camp that night was made in the tall brush a quarter mile or so from the creek. Frank had always maintained that when in strange or hostile country a man should not pick a spot too near a trail or stream, but make his stop a reasonable distance away, where he wasn't likely to be noticed by passersby.

Frank ... With the approaching of night the deep ache within her once again made itself felt. The remembrance of things he had said or done would keep coming to mind, and despite Fortuna's determination to be strong and self-sufficient, there were times in the silence of the night that she gave way to tears.

But with the ending of darkness her resolute vow to bring the outlaw killers to justice pushed back into her mind, even as the sunlight spread across the land, and she was quickly up and anxious to resume the trail.

Late that day she spotted the smoke of a camp along the creek a considerable distance ahead. Hope surged through her at the possibility it could be Pearson and the two outlaws with him— all taking it easy, and confident that any pursuit was far from getting underway.

Immediately Fortuna swung off the trail, forded the creek, and moved hurriedly down its west side as a means for concealing her presence. Keeping an eye on the thick plume of smoke, she continued until it would appear she was no more than a dozen yards from the camp, and there recrossed the stream.

Pulling to a halt in the tangle of heavy brush that grew along the water, Fortuna worked her way to the outer edge of the rank growth, and there, hunched low, put her attention on the camp.

A frown pulled at her tense features. She could see but two men—but reasoned at once that this was no proof there could not be a third somewhere out of view. She tried to locate the horses, determine if there were three—one a pinto—but the animals were picketed back in the brush, and not visible.

She had no alternative but to move in closer. Dropping back into the brush, Fortuna began to work her way nearer to the camp.

CHAPTER 8

Neither of the two men was Red Pearson—of that Fortuna was certain. But the pair could be Stringer and Benjamin. With their backs partly to her, and the fact she'd never had a good look at the red-haired outlaw's friends, she could make no positive identification. Assuming they were, however, it was only logical to believe that Pearson was nearby.

Fortuna, now less than a dozen yards from the two figures hunched by the fire apparently drinking coffee, hesitated. In her anxiety to overtake and bring to hand the killers she could be building something out of nothing. It was easily possible, she had to admit as she drew herself in behind the thick clump of rabbit brush where she had paused. The smart thing to do was to stay right where she was, keep an eye on the camp until she was certain it was, or was not, the outlaw party. Then—

"Just raise your hands, friend—less'n you want me to blow a hole in your guts."

Fortuna froze at the harsh command. Fear and

69

anger at her own carelessness rushed through her as she slowly began to lift her arms. She had caught the faint sound of a stealthy step behind her just as the grating voice broke the hush, and she felt the hard, round muzzle of a pistol or rifle barrel dig into her back. By then it had been too late to react.

"Now, start walking—and don't try nothing—"

Fortuna still could not see who the man was that was prodding her roughly toward the camp, but she didn't think it was Pearson. The red-haired outlaw had been in the Whitehill jail for something over a week, and she had heard his voice several times.

"What've you got there, Ollie?" one of the pair near the fire called out, coming to his feet.

"Ain't sure. Thought it was a danged Indian, him skulking around like he was, but I ain't never seen one before with red hair."

Fortuna, lips tight, halted before the men in the camp. She had been stupid, careless—had left herself wide open to being taken unawares. It was a bitter realization.

"Hell—I ain't sure it's a he!" one of the pair at the fire declared, leaning forward for a closer look. About thirty, he wore dirty, worn clothing, and even from the distance had a sour smell about him.

Ollie, the man holding the weapon to her spine, moved a bit to one side. Then: "By hell, Aaron, I'm betting you're right!"

Fortuna, thrusting aside the fear that gripped

her, and regaining her presence of mind, half turned to face Ollie.

"Put that gun away, damn you!" she snapped. "I'm a deputy marshal looking for three outlaws. Saw your camp, thought maybe you were them."

She felt the muzzle of the gun pressing into her back relent. Aaron glanced to the man beside him, and wagged his head. "Well, now, don't that beat all? Gabe, you ever come across a lady lawman before?"

Gabe, probably the youngest of the three, but equally dirty and foul smelling, grinned. "No, sir, I sure ain't never seen no female marshal!"

"You have now!" Fortuna stated, flat and unyielding. She drew aside the front of her jacket to reveal the star she was wearing.

Aaron whistled softly. "She's got herself a tin badge, all right! I used to have one just like it. Bought it for two bits from a peddler—"

"This one's real," Fortuna cut in. "Now, listen to me. One of the outlaws I'm hunting is riding a pinto horse. Fairly big man with red hair."

"Just like you, eh?" Ollie said, and reaching up tugged at a strand of hair that had worked itself loose from beneath her hat.

Fortuna jerked away angrily. She was up against another Jubal, it would seem, but she'd not allow herself to be backed down this time.

"Be enough of that!" she said curtly. "You see the man I'm talking about?"

Aaron scratched at his matted beard. "Well,

now, maybe we did, and maybe we didn't," he replied in a teasing voice.

"That ain't no way to answer the law!" Ollie said, shaking his head reprovingly. "This here's a genuine deputy marshal we're talking to, and we got to show some respect. Them fellows you're looking for, Deputy, are a far piece down the trail—but it's too late to go after them now. Smart thing for you to do is camp right here with us tonight, then light out after them in the morning."

"That's a real good idea," Gabe said, his eyes brightening. "We'd sure like some company—the female kind."

"Obliged, but I'll be moving on," Fortuna said, and started to turn away.

Instantly Ollie seized her by the hand. Pivoting, he swung her hard into Gabe and Aaron. Off balance from the collision, she rocked to one side, and into Ollie now closing in. He grabbed her again by the hand, whirled her once more at his partners. It was Gabe who caught her. Spinning her about, he threw her to the ground.

"She's mine!" Ollie yelled. "Was me that found her!"

As the man rushed toward her, Fortuna, collecting her confused senses, rolled to one side. Drawing her pistol she fired straight into Ollie's sweaty, grimy face. It disappeared into a blur of blood and smoke as the man was hurled away and down.

A long, breathless moment of silence followed

while the echoes of the gunshot rolled across the land. And then Gabe yelled, and lunged for her.

"Damn you—you slut! You've gone and killed Ollie! Was no need—"

Fortuna, a cold sort of fury flowing through her, rolled again, this time came to her feet, and avoided the man's rush. She had no wish to use her gun again, but would if it became necessary.

"Back off!" she ordered tersely.

In those soaring moments of excitement and danger she had proved herself, had discovered she was equal to the test—that she could kill a man if it was necessary.

"I ain't about to!" Aaron shouted, his mouth working angrily. "Time I'm done with you—you'll be wishing you'd never been born! Grab her, Gabe!"

The men closed in quickly. Fortuna jerked away from Gabe, felt Aaron's fingers wrap about her arm. Twisting, she brought up her knee and drove it into the man's crotch. Aaron cursed in pain, doubled over, and began to back away, his eyes wild as he gasped for breath.

Coolly Fortuna turned to Gabe. "You got any notions?" she asked in a quiet voice.

Inwardly Fortuna was in turmoil. Her stomach seemed to be in a tight knot, and something was clawing at her throat, threatening to shut off her breathing, but she permitted none of it to show.

Gabe had come to a sudden halt. He threw a hasty glance at Ollie's lifeless body, at Aaron now on his knees moaning softly.

"No, ma'am, I ain't thinking nothing," he answered hurriedly.

Tension began to fade from Fortuna as the turbulence within her slowly decreased. She motioned with the pistol she was holding.

"Get down on the ground—spread eagle."

Fear tore at Gabe's features. "You—you ain't figuring to kill me too, are you, ma'am?"

"Not if you do what I tell you—"

Immediately Gabe dropped flat on the warm sand, and stretched forth his legs and arms. Stepping up to him, Fortuna drew his pistol from its holster. Thrusting it under the waistband of her pants, she came about to Aaron.

"You, too."

Still holding his lower abdomen, Aaron stared up at her with hating eyes. He shook his head. "You hurt me real bad!"

"Nothing to what I'll do if you don't get down on your belly—like Gabe!"

Sullenly, Aaron complied. Fortuna removed his weapon from its belted case, retrieved Ollie's, dropped during the first moments of scuffling, and then placed her attention on Gabe.

"Where's your horses?"

She was fully in command now, totally confident, and knowing exactly what she would do, and how it must be done.

"Off there—in the brush," Gabe said, making an effort to point. "You ain't leaving us a'foot, are you, ma'am?"

"I am—long enough for me to be on my way.

You'll find your horses a mile or so down the creek. Guns will be in the saddlebags." Fortuna paused, studying Aaron's partly lifted head. "I don't think either one of you is stupid enough to follow me, but if you try it, you can figure to end up like your friend Ollie there—stone dead."

"We won't be following you—leastwise I won't," Gabe assured her.

"That'll show good sense. Same goes for Aaron. . . . Now, next time somebody shows you a lawman's star, respect it."

"Yes, ma'am."

Fortuna moved past the men into the brush, and locating the horses, freed them from the sapling to which they had been tied, and started back for her own mount. Gabe made no sound as she led the animals by him, but Aaron followed her with his glance, cursing steadily all the while. A hard smile was on her lips. She'd weathered the worst of incidents—and come out on top.

Reaching the sorrel and the gray, Fortuna dropped the pistols she had collected into the leather pouch on one of the confiscated horses. Mounting up, she led her small cavalcade back across the creek and turned south. It was near dark by the time she reached what she considered a suitable place to leave the horses, all of which looked as if they could use a night of rest and good grazing. Picketing them loosely, she continued on her way.

A distance later Fortuna, bearing in mind Frank West's admonition again, angled off from the stream, and made camp in a rocky arroyo a good mile to the west. There, suddenly drained mentally and tired physically, she built a small, well-hidden supper fire, prepared herself a simple meal, and then crawled into her blankets.

Tomorrow was another day, and with luck—assuming Ollie was to be believed—she would close in on Pearson and his outlaw pals. One thing was now certain in her mind: she was confident she could handle them.

CHAPTER 9

Fortuna awoke with a start. It was early morning, three or perhaps four o'clock, she thought as she lay perfectly still in her blankets. Something had brought her out of a sound sleep—a noise, or possibly it was intuition.

Ignoring the fear trickling through her, she continued to lie quietly, eyes partly open, waiting, until she knew what had awakened her. It was a precaution Frank West or no one else had told her of; it was ingrained, natural, and came from living in a country where strange, unaccountable noises could mean trouble.

Unmoving, her narrowed gaze fixed on the stars peering down at her from the dark heavens through the leaves of overhanging brush, Fortuna strained to hear the sound again. It came almost at once—a slight rustling in the brush. Fortuna's hand beneath the woolen covers slid to where she had placed her pistol. Taking a firm hold on it, immediately aware of the reassurance the weapon gave her, she resumed her pretense.

The noise had come from a few paces off to the

left and behind her. It could be an animal, she reasoned; one curious about the camp, perhaps seeking food, or simply attracted by the unfamiliar sight and smell of human presence.

A sharp, definite crackling—this time off to the right—sent alarm surging through Fortuna. There was someone or something out there—more than one it would appear. Indians? She doubted that, just as she now couldn't believe it was an animal of some sort; neither would betray themselves by such a careless approach.

It could only be men—two at the least. Fortuna's thoughts went quickly to the trio she'd encountered earlier: Ollie, Gabe, and Aaron. Ollie was dead, probably buried by that hour if his friends had bothered to accord him such attention. It could be the remaining two. She had taken the precaution of relieving them of their weapons and horses, and then left the animals a distance from their camp.

Fortuna was realizing now that such consideration had been in error; she had been too easy on them. The guns should have been thrown off into the brush where they could not have been found, and the horses driven off, and turned loose.

Of course, it could be someone other than Aaron and Gabe. Doubtless there were other parties in the area. Hell—it could even be Red Pearson and his two outlaw companions! That likelihood brought a tightness to Fortuna's throat. If it were, the hunt had come to an end. A grimness filled her at the thought.

"Over there—under that bush." The voice was barely audible. "That's her."

Fear once again endeavored to flood through Fortuna. An insistent voice deep within her cried out for her to throw aside her blankets, leap to her feet, scream, and break the monstrous tension that had suddenly laid hold of her. But she ignored the demand, remembering who and what she was, and that she had a pistol in her hand that made her the equal of any intruder.

Taut, Fortuna listened, hearing the soft swish of a leafy branch swinging back into place, the muted sound of a heel striking a rock—the faint rustle of cloth. The fire was out, and there were only the stars and moon to shed light on the area, making visibility very poor. She must rely on sound alone when the moment came to act.

That gave rise to thought. What should she do? What could she do under such circumstances— two men, perhaps more, coming at her from different directions? How could she defend herself? Fortuna could find no answer, knew only that she would have to make the best of it—and hope to come through.

Abruptly a dark shape was standing at the foot of her blankets. A noise off to the right warned her of a second man.

"Wake up, lady! You and me's got some mighty important business to tend to!"

Aaron! Recognition came instantly to Fortuna at the sound of the man's voice. It would be Gabe off in the brush to the right. In the next moment she saw Aaron bend forward, arm outstretched, clawing fingers reaching for the woolen cover drawn over her.

"You went and killed old Ollie—now you got the same coming to you—after I'm done—"

Fortuna threw aside the blankets and came upright with the quickness of a cat. The pistol in her hand blasted, filling the night with a vivid flash of fire and a chain of rocking echoes. Aaron yelled in surprise and pain, staggered back, dropping the weapon he was holding.

Another blast broke the darkness, adding more echoes to the still rolling chain. Gabe! Fortuna felt a bullet lay its searing course across her neck. She pivoted, bent low, triggered a second shot at the shadowy figure lurching toward her. Gabe paused abruptly, spun, and went to his knees.

"Don't shoot again!" he yelled. "I'm hit!"

Fortuna swore savagely under her breath, releasing the pent-up anger trapped within her. She had damn near got herself killed—all because she had figured Gabe was not the kind of man who'd take part in an attack on her—a conclusion she'd come to after their first encounter. She'd been wrong—he was no different from Ollie or Aaron. When in the hell was she going to learn that damn few men could be trusted? She'd let both Gabe and Aaron go, taking only minor precautions against them, certain they'd not bother her a second time.

Hell—she should have known Aaron's pride

would not let him rest after what she'd done to him, that he would come looking for her to even the score and recover his self-esteem. By God— she'd not make the mistake of being softhearted again!

Pistol still in her hand, and ready, she turned and crossed to where Gabe, clutching a bleeding shoulder, was hunched on his knees. Ignoring the man, Fortuna reached down, retrieved his pistol where it had dropped, and coming about, hurled it as far off into the brush as strength permitted.

"Ma'am, I'm sure hoping you—"

Fortuna, turning a deaf ear to Gabe, moved to where Aaron lay. His chest was covered with blood from the wound her bullet had made. She bent lower over him. There was a slackness to his bearded face that had taken on an ashen color in the pale light. Aaron was dead, or very near to it. A shudder went through Fortuna. She had killed another man, shot a third!

It was unbelievable—just as the change in her was also incredible. She was acting as a man— thinking, cursing, and using a gun to kill just as one would. Was that good or bad? Fortuna shrugged off the question. She had done what was necessary; the right or wrong of it was something she'd decide later.

Picking up Aaron's pistol, she threw it off into the brush also, and then collecting her gear she loaded up the gray pack horse and made ready to leave. Gabe watched her every move, moaning and groaning pitifully continually. She ignored

him, and when all was ready swung up into the
saddle of the sorrel. Taking the lead rope of the
pack horse, she started back to the trail.

"You just ain't leaving me here—shot bad and
bleeding like I am, are you, ma'am?"

There was appeal in Gabe's voice, but it was
lost on Fortuna West.

"Just what I'm doing," she replied callously,
and rode on.

Hours later Fortuna halted in a shallow wash
that paralleled the creek, and prepared herself a
light breakfast. She really wasn't hungry; a sort
of tremor still flowed through her—a memento of
the encounter with Aaron and Gabe—stifling her
appetite.

She had stopped but once during that period,
and that only long enough to wet her bandanna
in the stream and apply it to the place on her
neck where Gabe's bullet had left its mark. It
was a wound that scarcely could be called such;
the speeding bit of lead had drawn only a few
drops of blood in its passage, but it did sting.
Mounting up after that bit of personal attention,
Fortuna smiled as she recalled a remark Frank
had made once after having experienced a similar incident. *One of the best feelings in the world
is getting shot at, and missed,* he'd said.

Fortuna wondered if men ever got used to
killing. Frank, she knew, had been forced on
several occasions to shoot down an outlaw. It was
something he'd never talk about, however. He

just kept it inside himself until finally, with time, it faded into the past.

She could understand that now, but somehow to her it seemed a better idea to talk about it, get it out in the open, and put all the reasons for having done it into spoken words even though a person was alone. She tried it out as the sorrel moved steadily along when they were again on the trail, and found that it helped some.

It brought up another question, however; did that indicate a weakness? Was she still thinking and reacting like a woman, or was she—a woman —just better at the job of killing than a man?

How had Red Pearson, and Ike Stringer, and Tom Benjamin felt when they gunned down Frank? Had it bothered them—worthless, outlaw trash that they were—to murder a good, honest man?

Killing someone like them, or Ollie and Aaron, was one thing; and while taking any life was probably wrong, to kill a man like Frank West was not only a terrible crime, but a waste! Anger ripped through Fortuna again just as it did each time she thought of her husband's murder. She would need no provocation to gun down Pearson and his partners—and kill them without a moment's consideration she would when the opportunity came.

Shaking off her bitter reflections, Fortuna looked ahead. She had followed the trail along the creek since moving out that morning, and with the sun bearing down on her right shoulder, knew she

was still riding southward, the direction the outlaws were taking—apparently with the intention
of eventually crossing over the border into Mexico.

Eventually . . . Fortuna rolled the word about in
her mind. As near as she could remember from
the map that hung in Frank's office, Mexico was
well below Texas at this point. Most men plan-
ning to cross the border for one reason or another
preferred to head for El Paso, which was a much
nearer exit.

Weren't Pearson and his friends aware of that?
If so, was it possible she was on the wrong trail?
Had they cut away from the route along the
creek that she assumed they were following, and
turned to an angling course that would get them
to the Texas-Mexico border settlement much
sooner?

Disturbed by the thought, Fortuna at once cut
back to the east side of the stream, and rejoined
the trail. Walking the sorrel gelding slowly, she
kept her eyes on the occasional patches of soft,
loose soil until finally she spotted evidence of
where three horses had swung off to the right
and halted next to the stream where they apparently spent some time.

She couldn't be absolutely positive, of course,
but she was certain the party was Pearson's, that
he had paused there long enough to rest and
water the horses, and then ridden on.

She was still on the right track, Fortuna
concluded, but for how long? What was to keep
the outlaws, either aware of the shorter route or

learning of it from someone along the way, from changing course and heading for El Paso, and its counterpart across the Rio Grande, Juarez?

Nothing, Fortuna realized, resuming her saddle. And she had a strong feeling—a hunch—the outlaws had in mind to go to El Paso. It was a hunch—no more than that—but it brought to mind again what Frank had told her about the wisdom of obeying them.

Fortuna gave it careful consideration and came to a decision. She'd bank on her hunch, start cutting across open country for El Paso right then and there. Chances were there was a trail farther south that intersected the one following the creek, which led to the border city; and if she struck out now the likelihood of getting ahead of and waiting for Pearson and the others was good.

There was, of course, the danger that the outlaws would maintain a due south course, crossing that lower part of Texas on their way to the sanctuary they expected to find in Mexico. But Fortuna had doubts of that; Pearson had carefully planned the ambush and escape, and would just as carefully choose the route that would get him and his partners across the border.

Fortuna cut back across the stream, drew to a stop, and looked out over the broad plain rolling indefinitely on toward the west. There was little vegetation to break the sameness—yellowing bunch grass, occasional clusters of trees where there was a spring or a sinkhole in which water would collect during one of the infrequent rains,

snakeweed, grotesque cholla cactus, and nothing
more.

The very bleakness of the country convinced
Fortuna all the more of a cross trail intersecting
the one that followed Sulphur Creek somewhere
farther on south. Pilgrims no doubt would stick
to the much cooler route where water was available as long as possible before finally turning
west and undertaking to cross what appeared to
be little more than a desert.

Dismounting again, Fortuna watered the horses
and refilled her canteen. Although it was late in
the day she was anxious to move on, to get as far
along as possible before halting for the night.
Ready, she mounted the sorrel, and taking her
bearings from the sun, left the stream on a southwesterly course. She had no exact idea where the
town of El Paso lay, but reckoned once she came
to the anticipated trail or road that would be
running east to west, she had but to turn onto it,
and bearing right, follow it to the settlement.

But this was not exactly her intention. Reaching the east-west route she would halt, and taking a leaf from Red Pearson's book, set up an
ambush of her own. Then, when the outlaws appeared she would—

Fortuna's thoughts broke off. Slowing the sorrel,
she shaded her eyes with a hand, squinting into
the hovering haze. A dozen riders were coming
toward her. They were well into the distance, but
there was no mistaking their identity. Indians.

CHAPTER 10

"We're Kansas folk," Red Pearson said, smiling in friendly fashion at the young cowhand. "Going to Mexico. Aim to buy us a herd of cattle. Name's Jones. My partners there are Jackson and Smith."

"I'm Jim Converse," the cowhand said soberly, extending his hand. "I'm proud to meet you."

"Same here," Red replied. "You care for a swallow of liquor? It's pretty fair drinking stuff we bought over Fort Worth way."

"Don't mind if I do," Converse said, and accepting the half-empty bottle of whiskey, took a long drink. Returning the container he nodded, brushing at his mouth with the back of a hand.

"Dang good liquor all right! Sure beats that red-eye I've been getting over in Socorro."

"Socorro? Where's that?" Benjamin asked, hooking a leg over the horn of his saddle, and rolling a cigarette.

"Little town over on the Rio Grande—"

"Anywheres near El Paso?"

"Nope, it ain't less'n you figure a couple of hundred miles is near."

Pearson laughed. "I don't, that's for sure. This damn hill I'm setting on gets harder every minute."

Converse grinned, letting his hopeful glance touch the bottle of whiskey.

"Where are you headed, Jim?" Stringer asked.

"No place special. Got some folks in Austin. Had it in mind to drop by their place, put up for a few days, then sort of drift on. . . . That sure is a handsome paint you're riding, Mr. Jones. Don't see many of them around here unless there's a redskin a'straddle of it."

"Good horse," Pearson said. "I reckon we're on the right trail for this here El Paso—that's where we figure to cross over the border."

"It's the closest for sure. Just keep going the way you are, and you'll come to a crossroad. Take the right-hand fork—goes right straight to El Paso. Could take a shortcut, howsomever, if you're of a mind. Kind of mean going. Just head west across the flats."

"How much farther to that crossroad?" Stringer asked, brushing at the sweat glistening on his forehead. The sun was just past high center, and the heat was intense.

"Couple of days if a man rides easy. Maybe only half that if he pushed his horse real hard. . . . You reckon I could make another pass at that whiskey? Got a mighty long way to go waiting for me, and don't figure to come across any more drinking liquor like that for quite a spell."

"Sure," Pearson said, leaning forward in his

saddle, and handing the bottle to Converse. "Just help yourself."

The cowhand took several swallows, smacked appreciatively, and returned the now almost empty container to the outlaw.

"Sure am obliged to you fellows. Was a real pleasure meeting you," he said, wheeling his horse about, and starting to move off. "Good luck."

"Good luck yourself," Ike Stringer said, and drawing his pistol, put a bullet in the young cowhand's back.

Converse rocked forward from the impact of the heavy caliber bullet and caught at the saddle horn to keep from falling as his horse shied. Twisting around, his face contorted into a pain-filled, puzzled frown, he stared at Stringer—who was calmly reloading his weapon.

"Now, what'd you want to go and do that for?" the younger man asked plaintively, and then suddenly stiffening, pitched from his horse, and lay quiet on the sun-baked ground.

Stringer holstered his weapon; his cold, gray eyes empty, he briefly considered the lifeless, crumpled shape of Jim Converse.

"I reckon he won't go carrying no tales about us now," he said.

Red Pearson nodded, took a drink from the bottle of liquor, and passed it to Benjamin. "No, he sure won't. Kind of hate it, too. Seemed like a right nice young fellow."

" 'Cepting he had a mouth," Stringer said, awaiting his turn at the diminishing contents of the bottle. "First tin star he come across who asked him if he'd seen anybody down this way, he'd told him about three fellows heading for Mexico—and one of them riding a pinto horse. That'd be all the law'd need to get on our tails.'"

"Probably—but I reckon they'd been too late. We'd be in Mexico by then," Benjamin said as they moved on, still following the trail along the creek.

"Well, I ain't much for gambling on something like that," Stringer said. "This El Paso town could have one of them telegraph places, and whoever Converse would've talked to might high-tailed to where he could send a message saying we were coming that way. Now, with all that gold waiting for me to spend down in Mexico, I sure don't favor no welcoming party looking to grab me before we get there."

Benjamin nodded his agreement. "Just never thought none about that telegram thing. Red, you reckon it'd be smart to take that shortcut Converse told us about?"

Pearson shrugged. The heat and the liquor had turned him quiet. Slack in the saddle, he was paying little attention to what was being said.

"Shortcut?" he repeated. "Naw, we don't want that. Means taking out across open country. Could be spotted easy if there is somebody on our trail— which I'm damn sure there ain't."

"No sign of it," Benjamin agreed, and spat into the dust at the side of the road. "We sure can't get to Mexico any too soon, far as I'm concerned."

"Me neither," Stringer said. "I'm going to live high on the hog, I can tell you! Aim to get me a couple of them pretty Mexican señoritas, and have them just standing around waiting on me, and doing everything I want them to. What're you figuring to do with your share, Tom?"

Benjamin pulled off his hat and ran a hand through his dark hair. The sweat plastering his skin caused the scar on his neck to look raw and fresh.

"Ain't made up my mind yet—just never been much of a hand to skin a rabbit before he's caught, but if it all works out like we figure I think I'll buy me a little saloon somewhere, and get in the whiskey business. With my share of the gold— close to seven thousand dollars the way I calculate it—I can set myself up real good, and—"

"Five thousand," Red Pearson cut in bluntly.

Benjamin drew on his hat, frowned, and stared at the red-haired outlaw. "Five! Damn it all, you told me and Ike we'd divvy it three ways—after we got shed of that two-bit deputy!"

"Share and share alike," Stringer added in a tight voice. "That's the deal you made with us if we'd bushwhack them marshals so's you could get loose."

Pearson shifted his position on the saddle. "Maybe so, but I got to thinking about it later. Was no big thing to just open up on West and his deputy. Hell, they didn't even draw iron on you. With me getting the gold it was different. I had to stop that stagecoach—me and Turley together—

shoot it out with a couple of the guards before we could get to the strong box. Turley even got hisself killed doing it. I could've, too, only I was a bit smarter."

"And maybe luckier," Benjamin said dryly, and then added: "You'd be rotting in the pen right now if me and Ike hadn't come along, and all that gold would've wound up in the bank it was headed for."

"That's right," Stringer said, nodding. "You'd have flat out nothing if it wasn't for Tom and me."

"Can say the same for you two," Pearson countered coolly. "Wasn't for me hiring you, sort of, you'd still be rolling drunks, and sticking up—"

"That ain't no way to look at it, Red!" Tom Benjamin protested angrily. "We had us a deal, and now you're trying to back out." The outlaw paused, glancing at Stringer. "What do you say we pull up right here and now, and divvy up the money?"

"Three ways, like you promised, Red," Stringer reminded. "I'd feel a hell of a lot better if I was toting my share."

"Ain't no hurry," Pearson said, shrugging. "It's real safe where it is in my saddlebags. Can talk about divvying it up later—tonight maybe."

"We getting what you promised—a third for each of us?" Benjamin pressed.

Pearson's shoulders stirred again. "Well, I'll do some studying on it. Could be I will."

"Now you're talking straight!" Ike Stringer

declared. "Expect you was just funning us all along, saying you didn't aim to stand by your word."

Red Pearson glanced at the gunman, and grinned slightly. "Yeh, guess I was funning. Anyways, we'll straighten it all out later—like I said."

It didn't cost anything to play it smart, Pearson was thinking. He'd keep Ike and Tom Benjamin with him for protection until he got near El Paso, where he'd no longer have a need for them. That's when he'd settle up; two quick bullets, and there'd no longer be any question about how to divide the gold: it would all be his.

CHAPTER 11

Despite the self-confidence that had grown within her in the past few days something very like panic gripped Fortuna at the sight of the approaching Indians. She had heard how they treated the white women who were unfortunate enough to fall into their hands, and Frank had warned her to be ever on guard against them—emphasizing his point by relating an incident where he, unable to do anything about it, had witnessed the torture and death of an immigrant woman.

Abruptly giving way to fear Fortuna whipped the sorrel around and headed back for the trees and brush along the creek, driven by the urgent need to get out of sight. A fairly deep arroyo appeared. At once she rode down into it, all but dragging the stumbling pack horse after her.

Twisting about, she looked back at the Indians, wondering if by a stroke of good fortune they had not seen her. The party seemed to be moving at the same pace, and hope lifted within her that somehow she had escaped their notice. After all she'd been out on the open flat for only a few minutes, and this could be possible.

Too, not all redmen were bad. Most tribes were friendly and at peace with the government and settlers, although there were those who still felt the coming of the white people into what they considered their country was a cause for depredation and war.

It was those factions and the small bands of renegades that were a source of trouble—but the problem, Frank had said, was you never knew for certain which kind you were up against until maybe it was too late. The best thing, he advised pilgrims who stopped by his office seeking advice, was to avoid all Indians whenever possible; but if that could not be done, then be on guard, and ready to fight.

Fortuna followed out the wash until it began to curve west. At that point she came up to ground level, and using her spurs, drove hard for a grove of trees growing on the yonder side of the creek—a quarter mile or so distant. Again she flung a glance back onto the flats. The Indians, who had not altered course, were still coming toward her, at a faster pace she thought.

Reaching the stream and the brush that grew along it like a scraggly gray-green wall, Fortuna plunged recklessly into it. A sigh escaped her compressed lips. At least the Indians could no longer see her. Fording the creek, she broke out onto the trail on its opposite side, looking hurriedly about for a place to hide.

The grove of trees she'd spotted was still a distance farther on, and a bit to the east. Now calm, she spurred the sorrel, and struck for the grove, a stand of cottonwoods, sycamores, and scrub oaks laced with thick brush. As she reached it she drew once more to a halt, the question of where best to hide now foremost in her mind.

Probing about with her eyes she saw the crumbling adobe walls of a house and guessed the oasis had once been the site of a ranch or homestead—or possibly a way station for some stage line. In the deepening shadows of the afternoon she could see indications of other disintegrating structures, including one that looked fairly intact. Somewhere close by, judging from the plentiful growth, there would be a spring or creek.

Would this be a good and safe place to hide? Fortuna pondered the question, deciding it would not. Undoubtedly the Indians knew of the abandoned buildings, and if they had not spotted her, and were following the trail left by her horses, they probably would pull up there for night camp. She would be much safer well into the grove, and a distance farther on.

Avoiding open ground as much as possible to avoid leaving a clearer trail, Fortuna, senses sharpened by danger, continued on through the trees to the extreme southern end of the grove before she drew to a stop. The old way station structures, or whatever they were, now stood at the opposite side of the forested area from where she was.

The thought to push on—it was still not fully dark, and well short of the hour when she ordinarily halted to make camp—occurred to her, and leaving the pack horse ground-reined, she rode to the fringe of the trees, and considered the country beyond. It was open land—flat, and with little growth as she'd seen earlier. If she undertook to go on she would at once put herself in a position of being seen by the Indians. Coming about, Fortuna returned to where the gray was waiting; it would be smart to stay in the grove and make camp among the brush and trees.

Riding deeper into what appeared a denser, wilder section along the south side of the grove, Fortuna continued until she found what looked to be a suitable place. She would not risk the usual night camp. She had made up her mind to that before halting. Supper would be only cold bread and meat, and perhaps a can of peaches—and water. It would be sheer stupidity to build a fire for coffee.

The horses she would keep close by, ready to move out at any moment. Like as not she was taking all such precautions for nothing, but Fortuna had enough respect—and fear—for the redmen, although she'd seen nor heard no more of them, to take nothing for granted.

Picketing the horses where they were well hidden in a stand of dense, shoulder-high growth, Fortuna ate her simple meal, and then taking one of the blankets, located a small, cleared place at the base of a cottonwood, and there, with the woolen cover wrapped about her against the advancing coolness of the night, she settled down. There'd be no sleep, she was certain, but she would rest.

Around midnight, while dozing, she came alert with a start. Something had disturbed the sorrel, had caused him to shy, and set up a crackling of brush. Fortuna rose at once, and pistol in hand, carefully made her way to the gelding, a half-dozen strides from where she had been sitting.

She found nothing to greatly alarm her. The sorrel had moved a bit from where she'd left him, had done so probably because of an animal of some kind passing nearby. Laying her hand on the horse's neck Fortuna comforted him by patting and rubbing for a bit, and then started back for the cottonwood.

She froze. In the pale light of the moon and stars, and through the lacework of brush she saw two Indians standing in the clearing. They were staring at the blanket she had dropped when she went to see about the sorrel.

Panic again threatened to overcome her. She felt her throat tighten and a tremor race through her body. And then, regaining her self-confidence, she reacted. Thrusting a hand into her jacket pocket to still any sound that might be made by her spurs placed there earlier, Fortuna wheeled silently and dropped further back into the trees, moving slowly, carefully, and keeping in the shadows.

It would have been easy to use her pistol on

the two half-naked braves, but the fact that they were there was proof that she had been seen on the flat, that they had tracked her into the grove, and the rest of the party searching for her would be close by. Gunshots would bring them instantly.

Guttural shouts went up from the clearing as the braves announced their find to the others. At once Fortuna heard the soft pad of running feet beyond her. Instantly she dropped to the ground, and drew herself in under a bush of some sort. Moments later a brave, summoned by the shouts of his friends, trotted by. Others were responding too. Fortuna could hear more movement in the brush as well as voices coming from different nearby points in the grove.

Waiting until she was certain the last of the Indians had reached the clearing, Fortuna crawled from under the overhanging bush. Tense, she glanced to where the braves had gathered. There were ten, possibly twelve of them, standing beneath the spreading limbs of the cottonwood. Some wore breech cloths only, others were in pants, and all were bare waisted. As she watched, one of the braves took up her blanket and draped it over his shoulders, all the while speaking in a guttural, explosive way.

A yell went up as a brave appeared leading the pack horse. As he entered the clearing several of the party closed in about the gray, and began to remove the items she had secured onto the pack saddle. Another of the Indians drew attention briefly when he yelled something, and pointed in the direction of the sorrel.

Fortuna waited to see no more. The braves had begun to move out of the clearing. The search for her was beginning. Fear crowded from her mind by the basic need for self-preservation, and crouching low, she worked her way deeper into the forest. A sickening truth had become evident to her: the Indians had her horses. She was afoot now in a land where a mount was necessary for life. And she had no supplies.

Without realizing it Fortuna moved in a circle, as she stole quietly through the brush and trees. She could hear the braves searching for her, taking no pains to conceal their location as they shouted back and forth and tramped through the clumps of bushes and similar growth. Abruptly she halted. Two braves appeared before her—no more than a half dozen yards away. They had stopped to listen. Moonlight, filtering down through the leafed-out branches of the tree under which they stood, dappled their dark skins, and gave them a weird, unearthly appearance.

Shortly they moved on, and Fortuna continued, now taking assurance from the fact that she was behind the braves as they searched for her. Motion off in the shadows to her right again sent fear racing through her. She stopped and took a deep breath of relief. It was the sorrel still picketed where she had left him. Farther to the left she could see the pack horse. He was in the clearing where he had been taken, but the pack saddle on his back was empty. The supplies, extra clothing, and such articles that he'd carried were scattered about on the ground nearby.

If she could get to the sorrel, Fortuna thought, she just might have a chance of getting clear of the Indians and succeeding, either double back to the north, or else strike out across the flats. She had no idea where the braves had left their horses, but they would be near—of that she was certain. And if she was seen or heard riding off pursuit would not be long in forming. Moving off through the grove would be equally risky. The Indians had scattered and could be anywhere.

Her best bet was to stay where she was, keeping as near the sorrel as possible. Eventually the braves would give up their search in the dark, and return to their camp where they would await daylight. If luck was with her an opportunity for escape might then be presented to her, one that would allow her to slip in, get the sorrel, and after leading him off a safe distance, mount up, and flee. She'd have to forget about the pack horse and her trail supplies, hoping that, if she did manage to get away, she could find a ranch or a town where she could purchase replacements.

If she escaped at all. Therein lay the problem, and realizing its seriousness, a grim determination came to her: if the braves found her they'd never take her alive. She'd fight them to a showdown—but save the last bullet for herself.

Glancing about, Fortuna looked for a good and safe place to conceal herself. Another cottonwood growing near the one beneath which she'd camped caught her attention. Fairly large, its branches were low and thick with broad, heavy leaves. It occurred to her then that the braves she had watched kept their eyes fixed on the ground and brush, never bothering to look up.

That was the solution. She'd climb the tree, hiding within its branches—and hope for a chance to get to the sorrel once the Indians had returned and settled down.

CHAPTER 12

Luttrel drew in the bay he was riding, and thoughtfully studied the country stretching out before him. He was on the trail that followed Sulphur Creek—the course taken by the red-haired woman wearing a deputy marshal's badge who had taken it upon herself to track down three outlaws.

There was no one in sight, and that fact brought a frown to Luttrel's hard-planed features. The woman—he'd learned from the man who had been with her, and with whom he'd had a long talk, that her name was Fortuna West—had ridden on after the near brawl in Gunfire despite being alone.

That had aroused Ben Luttrel's interest. Any of the women he'd ever known would have called it quits then and there—but not this Fortuna West who had been widowed by the men she was pursuing. Despite the manhandling she was subjected to in the Texas Rose saloon, and the loss of the deputy accompanying her, she had kept right on after the killers—riding out that very evening.

To his way of thinking she was one hell of a woman!

He'd found out that she'd handled matters differently in Mulehead, the next town. Evidently learning from what had taken place in the Texas Rose, she had walked right into the largest saloon, asked for and got the information she was seeking—if three outlaws, one riding a paint horse, had been there, and if so which trail did they take when they left.

There'd been no repeat of the reception she'd faced in Gunfire. The bartender in the Mulehead saloon said she had been all business, and although there were several hard cases on hand in the place at the time not one of them had poked fun at her, or challenged the deputy marshal's star she was wearing.

It was at that point Ben Luttrel decided his trip to Fort Worth could wait. He had to see how Fortuna West's search for the men who had slain her husband turned out—and lend her a hand, if necessary. There was no personal interest, he assured himself, although there was no denying Fortuna West was an attractive woman, being tall—almost as tall as he was, Ben recalled from standing next to her in the Texas Rose—well built, and with strong, handsome rather than beautiful features. It was hard to imagine a woman taking on the risky, thankless job of a lawman, but he reckoned if anyone could make a success of it, it would be her.

But now a thread of worry was making itself in

Luttrel's mind. He had ridden hard since leaving Mulehead, and it seemed he should have seen some indication of her by that hour. Of course the trail that followed Sulphur Creek was replete with sharp bends and turns, brush grown tall and thick, and fairly plentiful trees, all of which limited vision for any distance.

Several things could have happened to her, he realized. She could have caught up with the outlaws, and failed in her intention to make prisoners of them; she may have encountered other men, and gotten in trouble; and there was a better than even chance she could have run afoul of some of the renegade Commanches prowling the area. And a woman alone in their hands—

Luttrel came to attention, his eyes on a rider who had moved into view well in the distance. It was too far to tell much about the horseman, only that he had emerged from the brush growing along the creek, and would shortly disappear again as a bend in the stream cut him from sight.

Could it have been Fortuna West, and not a man as he had simply assumed? Luttrel rolled the question about in his head. He had no idea what kind of a horse the woman was riding—not that it would matter at the moment; the animal had been too far away to determine anything other than that it was of dark color.

Luttrel touched his bay with spurs, sending the big horse moving forward. There was only one way to find out who the rider was—if it was

Fortuna West or not—and that was to continue. In time he and whoever it was would meet.

Ben's second glimpse of the horseman an hour or so later heightened the concern on his dark features. The rider was doubled forward over his saddle as if wounded. He could tell that much, but could still make no identification.

It wasn't the woman deputy Luttrel saw a half hour or so later. The rider was a young man who had been shot in the shoulder, and had plugged the bleeding hole with his bandanna. His horse came to a stop as Ben Luttrel rode in blocking the trail, at which moment the wounded man raised his head to stare woodenly at Luttrel.

"Looks like you could use a bit of help," the older man said, helping the rider from the saddle. "We need to do a bit more for that hole in your hide—it's bleeding plenty."

The wounded rider groaned, muttered unintelligibly as Luttrel seated him on a nearby rock, and removed the soaked bandanna for a closer look at the injury.

"When'd this happen?"

The rider shook his head weakly. "I—I don't rightly recollect. Couple of days ago. I think—or maybe it was just yesterday. Who're you anyway?"

"Name's Luttrel—"

"I'm Gabe Ramsey. I know you?"

"Maybe, but I don't remember us ever meeting," Ben replied, turning to his horse. Taking an almost full-pint bottle of whiskey, and a clean rag from one of the saddlebags, he returned to Ramsey, and handed him the liquor.

"Take a couple of swallows—it ought to make you feel better—while I see what I can do about slowing down that bleeding."

As Gabe helped himself to the whiskey, grateful sounds coming from him after each gulp, Luttrel ripped the rag into strips, made a compress pad of one, and then bound it snugly into place with another. That completed, he took the liquor from the rider, and poured a generous amount onto the bandage where it could soak through and into the pad.

Gabe squirmed and cursed deeply as the alcohol seared the raw wound, but after a moment he settled back on the rock. His eyes wild, he reached for the now almost empty bottle.

"I got to have another swig of that—"

Luttrel surrendered the liquor to Gabe, waiting while the suffering rider downed another long drink. Then, "You run in luck with that bullet. A bit lower, and you'd had a hole in your lung, higher and your shoulder would've been busted. What—"

"You're damn right I was lucky!" Gabe declared in a rising voice. "My partners both got themselves killed. I come out with just this here hole in my hide."

"Who did it—Indians?"

"Nope, there's a bunch hanging around here all right, but a damned marshal was the one."

"Marshal?" Luttrel repeated. "A woman marshal?"

Gabe Ramsey swore, looked off toward the creek, and was silent. And then as if reluctant to admit it, said, "Yeh—was a woman. A red-headed one."

"She killed your partners—shot you?"

"Just what she done. That ain't no regular woman I'm talking about—this one's a regular hell cat!"

Luttrel suppressed a grin by rubbing his jaw. "What brought on the shooting?"

Gabe shrugged, and immediately winced at the pain. "Hell, it was just sort of a misunderstanding. Me and my friends, one was Ollie Gray, other'n was Aaron Bradly, was camped when this gal showed up. Fact is Ollie caught her sneaking in on us.

"Claimed she thought we was three other birds she was looking for—outlaws she said they was. We all figured it was a big windy—a gal chasing three killers all by herself. None of us believed it—"

"It was true," Luttrel broke in.

Gabe frowned, stirring in an effort to relieve the throbbing pain in his shoulder. "She a friend of your'n?"

"No, only seen her once—"

'Well, anyway, Ollie figured she was just some gal drifting around the country like us, so—well, we'd just keep her for the night, and we'd all have ourselves a good time. He grabbed her, and throwed her down. Next thing we all knew she'd shot him right in the head.

"Aaron got real mad at her for doing that, and tried to get a hold of her, too. She drove her knee into his privates, then took our guns and horses and rode off. When Aaron got hisself back together he was mad enough to bite a horseshoe. Said no lousy woman was going to get away with what she done to him. So we took off, found our horses and guns, and trailed her.

"That's when she killed Aaron—and plugged me. We found her camped and sleeping—only she wasn't. Tricked us. Was playing possum. When Aaron jerked off her blankets and started to crawl on her, she jumped up and shot him in the heart."

"How'd you get hit?"

"Well," Gabe said, again hesitating. "Was nothing I could do but take a crack at her after she killed Aaron. Missed—she was doing a lot of jumping around. She come right back at me with a shot that got me in the shoulder. Then she mounted up and rode off leaving Aaron there dead, and me bleeding to death."

Luttrel, handing the bottle with its small amount of whiskey remaining to Ramsey, drew himself erect from the crouch he had assumed.

"This all happen somewhere along the creek?"

"Yeh. Ten, maybe fifteen mile south of here. I ain't so sure about it—about nothing. Been sort of out of my head."

"You'll be all right now," Ben said, turning to his horse. "Keep riding up the stream, and you'll come to a town—Mulehead they call it. Find a doctor there. Think you can get yourself back in your saddle?"

"I reckon so," Gabe replied. "Sure obliged to you for the liquor—and for patching me up. You heading on south?"

Luttrel, on his horse, nodded. "Yeh—south."

"Well, you hear what I say. If you come across that female deputy, don't try nothing! She'd as soon shoot you as bat an eye."

"I'll take care," Luttrel replied, grinning as he cut the bay back onto the trail.

CHAPTER 13

Fortuna West, hunkering well above the ground in the crotch of the cottonwood, tensed as she heard a rustling below her. A moment later two of the Indian braves appeared in the small clearing, emerging from the brush like silent shadows.

For a brief time the two men talked back and forth, one taking up her blanket where it lay, and draping it about his naked shoulders. Then both began to collect the dry wood that lay strewn about, dropped it in the center of the open ground, and one taking a long bladed knife from the sheath slung at his side, and a bit of flint rock from a sack also hanging from his belt, started a fire.

The smoke lifting at once began to drift into the surrounding trees, and at once set up a fear in Fortuna. If the vagrant breeze should smoke the cottonwood where she had taken refuge she might give herself away by coughing. But so far the thick, blue haze appeared to be moving in the opposite direction.

Two more braves magically appeared in the camp and squatted by the fire. Shortly others appeared, some dragging or carrying in more fuel for the fire, now blazing brightly. Fortuna saw eleven braves in the party—all half-naked, copper-skinned, black-haired men well armed with rifles and knives.

Several began to probe about in her belongings that lay scattered about. One came upon the change of underwear she had brought along, and holding it against his body, began to dance around the fire, laughing and yelling. Others had discovered her stock of trail grub, were breaking open the sacks, cutting open the cans, and tasting their contents—which they either spat out, or continued to eat.

She noticed two off at the edge of the flaring firelight bent low examining a rifle. She recognized the rifle as hers and realized they had taken it from the boot on her saddle. Fortuna swore angrily. The rifle, a gift from Frank, was a prize to her. She hated like hell to lose it.

A wry grin pulled at her lips. It was getting to where she swore like a trooper! Often she'd wondered why men resorted to violent language in times of anger and stress; she was now beginning to understand. Trapped in a situation where nothing could be done, a good, solid round of cursing did relieve things.

Yells went up from the Indians moving about in the glow of the fire. Almost directly below her two of the braves were scuffling over a scarf she had brought along to use for tying down her hair in the event she encountered a windstorm. The men were each gripping an end of the scarf, struggling to pull it away from the other.

The tugging contest went on for several minutes during which the opponents rocked and staggered about, colliding with others in the party, all the while yelling at each other. Abruptly a brave, squatting to one side eating from the sack of hard biscuits Fortuna had brought along, rose to his feet. Drawing his knife, he stepped in close to the sweating, straining contestants and slashed the scarf into two pieces, effectively ending the ownership dispute.

Both braves, tension on the strip of cloth released, staggered back, one going down flat on his hindquarters while the other stumbled into a member of the party. Both recovered quickly, and shouting and gesturing angrily, charged across the clearing to where the third brave, knife back in its sheath, had settled back on his haunches and resumed eating. He did not bother to look up as the pair railed and ranted at him, only shrugging indifferently now and then.

Others had paused to watch and listen, some laughing and conversing in a quick, guttural tongue. Some of the words sounded like Spanish to Fortuna, but she had but little knowledge of that language, and none at all of the one used by the Indians which, she understood, varied from tribe to tribe. Frank had been well versed in them; she, however, had never really bothered.

Fortuna regretted that oversight, wishing she might have an idea of what the Indians planned to do. Were they intending to spend the night in the clearing, and resume the search for the person who belonged to the camp, a woman—a fact that was now undoubtedly clear to them from the articles of clothing they had found in the pack? Or would they consider one person not worth troubling with? After all, they had the horses and the rifle, which were most important to them. They should be satisfied.

Should they move out taking both the sorrel and the gray she would be left on foot—and miles from any settlement, insofar as she knew. Of course, there was the chance she'd encounter other pilgrims—parties like Ollie, and Gabe, and Aaron, who, while the lowest form of men, were still preferable she supposed to falling into the hands of renegade Indians.

Drawing the doeskin jacket closer about herself as protection from the advancing chill of the night, Fortuna shook her head in disbelief. A week ago she could not have imagined she would ever find herself in the situation she now was. Frank was alive, things were going smoothly, and she was concerned only with housewifely duties and other everyday occurrences. Life was, and had been, more or less a routine affair except when her husband took her with him hunting, or on lawman business to some nearby, or perhaps distant, town.

It was incredible. Here she was—an ordinary, church-going, peace-loving woman who had actually killed two men, and in all likelihood would take the lives of three more—perched in a tree in the middle of the night, like some frightened animal, while below her nearly a dozen Indians, aware of her being but unable to locate her, made sport of her belongings while they awaited dawn when they would resume their search.

At least that appeared to be what the braves had in mind, as about half of them had stretched out near the fire and were sleeping. Others still prowled about probing through the articles they'd removed from the pack saddle in hopes, apparently, of finding something of value or interest that they had missed earlier. The pack horse had been led back, and picketed near the sorrel, and the Indian ponies had been brought up, and were hobbled a short distance beyond.

The fire began to dwindle, shrinking the circular flare of light thrown by the flames. One of the braves disappeared into the brush, returned after a few moments, and picked up a large handful of dry limbs and forest litter. Throwing it all onto the fire, he stepped back, watching the flames spurt into vigorous life.

Two of the Indians who had been off to one side chewing on the dried beef they'd found in her pack rose, stretched, and lay down with the others,

one using the blanket she had dropped. She could
certainly use the woolen cover at that moment,
Fortuna thought; it was growing colder, and that,
combined with her cramped muscles, was making her miserable. But she could stand it—and
would. If she made any move to change her position in the tree the sound unquestionably would
draw swift attention—and then all would be over
for her.

Now only three of the braves were still awake.
They were hunched by the fire, carrying on a
conversation at low voice. Fortuna stared at them
numbly, wishing, hoping they would either sprawl
out in the warm glow of the campfire or find a
convenient tree where they could settle down,
backs to its trunk, and sleep, as had some of the
others.

From somewhere nearby an owl hooted plaintively. Or was it really an Indian—a stray losing
the party, and finding it now from the glare of
the fire? The trio below had ceased their talking
to listen. The sound came again. The Indians
resumed their conversing, evidently satisfied that
the complaint had come from a bird. Fortuna
sighed in relief; what she didn't need were more
braves showing up at that moment to arouse the
entire party.

The moments dragged by, becoming minutes
that grew into hours. The group of three braves
were no longer talking except in lagging, brief
spurts, but all continued to sit by the fire, each
now and then adding a bit of fuel to the flames. A

question came to Fortuna West's mind; had they been chosen to stay awake, to remain on guard as sentries, or whatever the Indian term might be? It would seem so; all of the others were sleeping soundly.

She was not sure how much longer she could remain in the cottonwood without changing position. Her entire body was aching, and a stiffness had overtaken her, setting up the worry that she could have difficulty in moving quietly when, and if, the time came to descend from the tree, get to the sorrel and make her escape.

Abruptly the hold-out braves got to their feet. Together they walked out of the circle of light into the brush, toward the ponies. She could see their silhouetted shapes moving about the horses, apparently making sure the animals were secure, and then all returned, found places near the fire, and lay down.

Relief and hope began to course through Fortuna. Controlling an impulse to rise, to straighten her cramped legs, she rode out another ten minutes, making certain none of the braves were awake. Finally convinced, she drew herself upright in the crotch of the cottonwood.

A feeling of release spread through her, but a sharp tingling now claimed her legs. Grasping the thick limb against which she was leaning Fortuna gritted her teeth and endured the prickling sensation until blood circulation had restored itself.

Taking a final, close look at the Indians to be certain none had aroused, and satisfied all were yet asleep, she began a tedious, careful descent of the tree, making certain her boots and other parts of her clothing did not scrape against the bark of the cottonwood, and set up a sound.

Almost down Fortuna caught herself. One of the braves had stirred and was sitting up. Motionless, breath locked in her throat, she watched him pick up a handful of sticks, and throw them onto the fire. That done, he lay back.

Clinging tight to the tree's trunk Fortuna stalled another dragging five minutes, and then finished lowering herself to the ground. Immediately, crouched low, she worked her way to the sorrel. She'd have to leave the pack horse, just as she would lose all of her trail supplies—and her rifle. She reckoned that was a small price to pay for escape—and her life.

Reaching the sorrel, Fortuna quietly freed the short piece of rope she'd used to tie the gelding to a sapling, and glanced about seeking the best way to leave—one where there would be a minimum of brush for the sorrel to rub against. Straight ahead looked to be the right choice. She would lead the animal for a fair distance away from the camp to a point where she was certain to be beyond earshot, and then halt, tighten the saddle cinch, and mount up.

Grasping the bridle of the sorrel to better lead him, Fortuna started to move off. A faint sound behind her sent her pulse racing. Instinctively she dropped a hand to the pistol on her hip, and wheeled.

An Indian was standing no more than an arm's length away.

CHAPTER 14

A chill swept through Fortuna, one that had no relation to the temperature of the night. Evidently she had betrayed herself with a sound, careful as she was, after all. It had aroused the brave, brought him to investigate. As startled as she, he stood before her, mouth open in surprise, eyes spread wide.

Her reaction was instantaneous. Anger flamed through her, and releasing her grip on the sorrel's headstall, she swung the pistol in her hand with all the strength she could muster.

The blow caught the brave just above the ear. He grunted, his knees buckled, and he began to sink. Again reacting Fortuna flung her arms about him to prevent his falling. This could make enough noise to bring some of the others. Holding the man's ill-smelling body close, she lowered him slowly to the ground, then straightening up she flung a glance at the clearing. The fire had died somewhat and most things in the camp were indistinct, but she could detect no movement among the deepening shadows.

Stepping quickly away from the unconscious brave, Fortuna again took the sorrel by the bridle, and began to move off into the brush. The first few yards went well, their passage being almost soundless, but a bit later the gelding clicked a shoe against a stone. The noise seemed to rise and echo, and reach out for miles in the silence, but Fortuna had the presence of mind to not halt or panic, but continue on at the same, cautious pace she was following.

A dozen yards ... twenty ... fifty. Fortuna halted, and stepping hurriedly to the gelding's side, hung the stirrups on the saddle horn, and pulled the cinch tight. Moments later she was astride the horse, and moving on now at a fast walk.

She kept to the brush, alert for any sounds of pursuit, circled, and eventually made her way back to Sulphur Creek from which she'd be able to take her bearings. Reaching it, and acting on impulse, she urged the gelding down into the hock-deep water, and pressed on. Should the Indians attempt to track her when daylight came such precaution should effectively block their efforts, she reasoned.

Fortuna was breathing easier now. She had taken a desperate chance, but it had worked out all right—she had escaped. Too, a bit of contention that had lain between her and Frank West was now better understood. She had scolded him on numerous occasions for taking what she considered unnecessary chances. He had endeavored to explain that he hadn't done so in the spirit of showing off, or just for the hell of it, but because it was the only choice open to him.

Concealing herself in a tree, climbing down from it when she judged it safe, and getting her horse had been the one course open to her, she realized, for to have remained there would have placed her in a most dangerous position. Frank had been right. There were times when taking a risk was the only way out of an otherwise hopeless situation.

Heading the sorrel up and out of the stream after a mile or so, Fortuna walked him to the edge of the brush, and swung from the saddle. She stood there in the shadow of a mesquite for a time listening, her eyes on the trail to the north. She could neither see nor hear any sign of the Indians.

Taking her spurs from the pocket of her jacket, Fortuna buckled them into place, and went back into the saddle. Putting the gelding into motion she continued southward, keeping as much in the brush as possible. She'd stay under cover until daylight; but then she should be far enough from the Indians to strike out across the flats to the west, and resume her hope of getting ahead of Red Pearson and the others as they rode for El Paso.

An hour later with the eastern sky beginning to brighten, the sorrel broke stride and slowed. Fortuna, dozing in the saddle, came bolt upright and pulled the gelding to a stop. A horse was standing in the center of the trail directly ahead, and slinking away from a body of a man that lay nearby were two coyotes.

Had it not been for the lean, little prairie wolves, Fortuna would have hesitated to halt, fearing it might be a trap of some kind, but with the scavenging pair there, there was no doubt in her mind that the figure she saw was that of a dead person. Moving in closer she dropped from the saddle, and knelt by the rider.

A cowhand, she guessed from his clothing, throttling the wave of nausea that struck her. He was still wearing a gun, and there was a bullet in his back, which was a clear indication that he had been taken from behind. How long he'd been dead Fortuna had no way of knowing. The body was stiff, showing considerable mutilation from vultures and the coyotes, which led her to believe the shooting had taken place at least the previous day.

Searching the man for identification, and finding none, Fortuna rose and glanced about. There was nothing to be done but drag the body off the trail, and bury it as best she could. There was no convenient wash close by to serve as a grave, as had been the case with Zeke Tyler, but there was a small hollow not far from the creek. Taking the corpse by the heels, Fortuna grimly pulled it into the shallow sink, and covered it over with brush and rocks. That done, she returned to the trail.

The rider's horse had moved up to stand beside the sorrel as if lonely, and seeking companionship.

She had no need for the animal, and could see no point in taking him with her so, removing the saddle and bridle and leaving them in the brush, she freed the horse that he might forage unhampered along the creek.

Once more mounted, Fortuna continued her southward course, wondering as she rode on through the chilly half light, how the young cowhand came to his death. It had not been the Indians, she was certain; they had come from the west, across the flats, and arrived at the stream well to the north. And she doubted it could have been Ollie, Gabe, and the third member of the party, Aaron. The killing had been too recent for them to have been involved.

Could it have been Red Pearson, or one of the outlaws with him, that had put a bullet in the cowhand's back? Time and location indicated this was possible, but why would they do it? The rider hardly could have posed a threat to them, and the fact that his pistol was still holstered would mean there was no argument in progress. Fortuna shrugged. Likely she'd never know who had pulled the trigger that sent a bullet ripping into the cowhand's back, and friends and relatives, if he had any, would forever wonder what had become of him.

It was not so difficult to kill, Fortuna realized. She'd wondered earlier if she had what it took to shoot a man, to take a life, and had found the answer when she was faced with protecting herself from the drifter, and later on his partner, Aaron.

There'd been no hesitation on her part in the act. She had simply drawn her weapon and fired, finding the actual shooting easy, and the aftermath of emotion practically unnoticeable. She had thought she might freeze when the instant came to trigger her pistol, and if successful in overcoming that, find herself submerged in a torrent of guilt and shame.

It had not been that way in either case. She had done what was necessary to preserve her life, and then dismissed it from her mind.

It would be like that when she finally caught up with the men who had killed her husband. She'd not hold back on shooting them down, just as they had shown no mercy when they murdered Frank. In fact, Fortuna realized she was looking forward to facing them.

Somewhere along the way a change had taken place within her, one that brought about a subtle altering of values. Her intentions—so firm in the beginning—to capture and make prisoners of the three outlaws and return them for the court's justice no longer occupied her mind. She would not wait for that now, would instead mete out the punishment they deserved herself, and thereby save time as well as insure that Pearson, Stringer, and Benjamin got what was due them.

Fortuna had learned she had the courage, the will, and the ability to use her pistol, and accordingly was capable of doing the job. All that remained now was the execution of it. She frowned, wincing at the word, not much liking its implication. Immediately she passed it off. As well she be the outlaws' executioner as some paid hangman.

Daylight broke in the east, spraying the sky with orange, pale reds, and yellows. The chill increased with the ending of night, and then began to fade even as did the shadows along the brush. Somewhere a meadowlark broke the early hush with its cheerful song that served at once to dispel some of the grimness filling Fortuna, and to lift her spirits.

It would be safe now to head out across the flats to the west, she decided. If her plan to get out ahead of Pearson and the others was to succeed—again assuming they were riding to El Paso—she should angle across the plain and reach the road they would be traveling as soon as possible. Hesitating no longer, she cut away from Sulphur Creek, and began the journey again— one interrupted earlier by the appearance of the Indians.

Around mid-afternoon a faint stirring of the weed clumps and occasional stands of brush came to her attention. The wind was rising, and more than likely at that time of year bringing with it a sandstorm. Fortuna sighed wearily. That was something she could do without although, if it were strong enough, it would effectively conceal her passage over the flats. Regardless, she thought impatiently, like the hunger that was beginning to make itself felt, there wasn't a damn thing she could do about it.

Ben Luttrel, holding his bay horse to a faster than ordinary lope, kept to the trail that followed meandering Sulphur Creek. At times it might have been wise to maintain a direct course rather than stick to the well-beaten track, but this would require the bay to pick his way through rocks, tall weeds, gullies, and tough underbrush, and in the end the shortcut would entail more time.

And Luttrel was anxious to overtake Fortuna West. His interest in the tall, red-haired woman had increased as the hours passed, and he thought more and more about her. He wondered, worriedly, if she realized who she was going up against— killers who would not hesitate to shoot her down. Being a woman would not count with them.

But she had held her own where Gabe Ramsey and his two friends were concerned, Ben had to admit. That, however, was a different breed of cat; they were nothing but trail tramps, saddle bums, the kind of loafers who hang around saloons looking for ways to steal a dollar, or anything else of value. They could not be put in the same class with the men who had killed Fortuna West's husband, all hardcase, experienced outlaws if the deputy who had accompanied her as far as Gunfire was to be believed, and there was no reason why he shouldn't.

Luttrel immediately swung the bay into the

brush on his right. A half dozen or more—nine to
be exact—Indians had emerged from the heavy
growth a hundred yards or so farther along. Riding single file, they hadn't seen him. Keeping
well back in the growth along the creek, he
watched them angle toward the low hills to the
east.

He stiffened. A worried frown pulled at his
dark features. One of the braves, the last in line,
was leading a horse with an empty pack saddle.
Could the animal be Fortuna West's? Had she
run into the Indians, and had trouble with them?

It was entirely possible. The party was in the
area where she could be. Tension eased slightly
in Luttrel. If true, the woman had evidently escaped from them, otherwise the braves would not
only have both of her horses, but Fortuna as well
with them.

Considering the way she had handled herself
with Gabe Ramsey and his partners, that seemed
logical. She had gotten away from the Indians
somehow, had lost the pack horse—and likely all
of her gear. This could result in her turning back
now, giving up the hunt. Or would it?

Luttrel brushed at the sweat on his dark face,
shrugged, and headed his horse across the creek
to the opposite side where he would not be visible
to the Indians. Fortuna hadn't quit at Gunfire,
and the incident with Ramsey and the men with
him hadn't stopped her. Ben had a strong hunch
that no matter what condition she was now in,
the lady lawman would keep going.

On the back side of the stream, and again pointing south, Luttrel raked the bay with his spurs, and put the horse to a gallop. He'd like to help Fortuna West; undoubtedly she was in need of a helping hand from somebody, but to do so he had first to catch up with her.

CHAPTER 15

Startled, Fortuna jerked her horse to a halt. An Indian, as if by magic, was standing before her blocking the trail. Apparently he had seen her coming, and had waited for her in the dense brush growing along both sides of the path.

Surprise and then frustration ran through her. She looked more closely at the brave—his copper body glistening with sweat, thin lips drawn back in a toothy grin. He was the one she'd buffaloed when making her escape from the camp. There was a swelling around his left temple as well as a trace of blood where her weapon had broken the skin.

Reacting quickly, Fortuna reached for the pistol on her hip. Indian men, like most white ones, had a stiff pride also, it would seem. The brave couldn't swallow being bested by a woman; he had ridden hard on the trail to get ahead of her and lie in wait. This time she'd fix him good— once and for all.

Her hand closed about the butt of the .44, finger hooking around the trigger as her thumb found the hammer. In the next moment Fortuna saw a second copper shape come hurtling out of the brush from her left. There were two braves! She attempted to throw herself to one side, failed as the Indian's arms went about her body, and clawing hands locked onto her clothing.

In the next fragment of time Fortuna felt herself being dragged from the shying sorrel. She struck the ground flat on her back, breath exploding gustily from her lungs. She heard both Indians yell as she again made a grab for her gun. Before she could bring it into play the brave who had pulled her from her horse—a heavy-set man wearing a dirty pair of white drawers and a red band around his head—knocked her hand away, seized the weapon, and placing a foot on her chest to pin her down, thrust the weapon under his waistband.

The brave Fortuna had bludgeoned into unconsciousness earlier came walking up, strutting a bit as he grinned down at her. The grin on his face had widened. He said something to his partner, and both laughed.

Fortuna, sucking for breath after being thrown so forcibly to the ground, and from the pressure of the squat brave's foot on her chest, looked about for any more members of the party. She could see no others, reckoned the pair were alone, having dropped back to search for her while the remainder of the Indians had continued on for wherever they had been bound.

The brave holding her down removed his foot, and with motions and guttural sounds commanded her to rise. Fortuna, taking her time, and striving to show no fear, did as she was bid.

The men, both grinning, began to circle her, looking her over carefully as a buyer might do a horse he intended to purchase. The one with the swollen head paused in front of her, reached out, and seized the lapel of her fringed jacket. Fortuna jerked away.

Both Indians laughed, exchanged words, and then the one with the red band about his head pointed into the brush, and motioned for her to move off ahead of them. Mind working furiously as she sought to come up with an idea for escaping, Fortuna did as she was told.

She came to a small clearing where two horses were standing. A hand fell on her shoulder, bringing her to a stop. She waited while the squat brave led her sorrel over to where their ponies had been picketed, after which he took time to go through her saddlebags. Finding nothing of interest he returned to where the first brave, evidently guarding her from making a break into the brush, was gingerly probing the place on the side of his head where she had struck him with his fingers.

He was of no great interest to Fortuna at the moment. The heavy-set brave was the one who had taken possession of her gun, and that was what she must have—either it or one of the rifles they had leaned against a nearby tree—to get away from them.

From a pouch hanging at his lean waist the Indian she had struck procured a coil of rawhide. Roughly pulling her hands behind her back, he bound Fortuna's wrists tightly together, and then pointing to the ground, indicated she was to be seated.

Fortuna did not move, stubbornly remaining where she was. The younger brave stepped forward, and raising an arm, slapped her sharply across the face. Tears sprang into Fortuna's eyes, and lights popped in her head. She staggered, went down. Both braves laughed as she fell against a tough, springy berry bush and, rocking awkwardly, was thrown forward. Turning then the braves crossed to the center of the clearing where they squatted on their heels, and began to converse.

Red Band glanced to the west, apparently judging the hour from the sun's position. They were discussing the question of whether to camp there for the night, or hurry on and overtake the rest of the party, Fortuna guessed. Evidently the former course was decided upon. Both got to their feet. Red Band hurried off into the brush while the younger man, collecting a supply of wood from the immediate vicinity, threw a quantity of it into the center of the open area, striking a spark to a bit of dry tinder. When a flame caught, he nursed it into full life, and then turning moved to where Fortuna sat. Taking a sitting position also, he crossed his legs, folded his arms across his chest, and began to stare morosely at her.

As the minutes had moved past, tension and fear within Fortuna had grown. She had no illusions as to what was in store for her, and was concentrating her thoughts and mind on a means of escape. Bound as she was she could see but a small chance. Now desperate, she put her full attention on the brave, and forced a smile to her lips.

"You got a name?" she asked in a friendly tone.

The Indian stared at her, sullen and unforgiving. She had made a fool of him in front of his friends—a woman, and this was impossible to bear.

"Me Comanche," he replied, not understanding.

"Comanche," Fortuna nodded. "What's your name? How are you called?"

The brave frowned, and then finally comprehending said, "Little Tree." He pointed a finger at her. "You?"

"Fortuna," the woman replied, and twisted half about to show her wrists. "Too tight. Hurt."

Little Tree considered her blankly. Again Fortuna displayed her bound wrists. "Tight. Hurts."

The brave nodded, finally understanding. Fortuna tensed. If she could get the Indian to release her hands she might get a chance to lunge against him, knock him down, and get to one of the rifles. With a weapon Fortuna felt she'd then be equal to any problem.

Little Tree pulled himself erect, and started toward her. A shout from the edge of the clearing brought him to a stop. Red Band, a rabbit dangling from one hand, a bird of some kind from the other, padded into view. The stocky brave held up his prizes for Little Tree to see—he evidently was indicating their supper. Fortuna knew then why he had left the camp; he had gone to the stream where birds and animals watered to hunt, and had succeeded.

Little Tree wheeled and crossed to the fire. With his knife he cut two sticks with forks at one end, sharp points at the other. Thrusting the latter into the ground at either side of the fire, now a glowing bed of coals, he then fashioned a third stick into a crosspiece. While he was preparing the spit Red Band had skinned and gutted the rabbit; with the bird he was satisfied to rip off most of the feathers taking no pains to pluck it clean or to remove its inner organs. Taking the crosspiece Little Tree had prepared, the brave thrust it through the two carcasses, and placed it in the forks of the uprights, thus suspending the intended meal over the fire. That accomplished, he added a small amount of wood to the coals, and as the flames burst into life, stepped back. Rubbing his hands together he glanced at Fortuna, gestured, and said something.

Little Tree shifted his attention to her, and made his reply. Hope sagged in Fortuna. A good opportunity, perhaps her only one, to escape had been lost when Red Band had returned. Feeling the heavy drag of despondency she sank back, shoulders against the resisting berry bush, and stared unseeingly at the braves.

They were squatting near the fire. Red Band was revolving the crosspiece of the spit slowly, allowing the rabbit and the bird, whatever it was, to cook evenly. He was maintaining a steady conversation with Little Tree whose part in the preparation of the meal seemed to be one of feeding the fire a small amount at a time.

The minutes began to drag by for Fortuna. She had not given up hope of escape entirely, but rake her brain as she would, she could still see no way out of the tight spot she found herself in. Fortuna glanced nervously at the sun. Only a couple of hours or so of daylight remained. She feared the coming of darkness, yet welcomed it for it would lend concealment if she, somehow, could get away from the renegade braves and what she knew they had in store for her.

The rabbit and the bird were finally cooked. Red Band removed the crosspiece from its supporting forks, and extended it rabbit foremost to Little Tree. The younger brave, taking his knife, slid the small animal off the length of wood, muttering when it burned his fingers, and laid it on a nearby rock. The bird Red Band claimed for himself. Handling it gingerly, he began to eat, tearing the small morsel apart with his teeth while ignoring the heat, and making loud smacking noises as he ate.

Little Tree speared the rabbit with his knife,

and transferring it to his free hand, put the blade aside. Taking one of the hind legs of the animal in his fingers, he tore it from the carcass. Twisting about he called, "Fortuna," and tossed the bit of meat to her. It fell close by, gathering a coating of dirt and bits of litter as it did.

Anger swept her. They were treating her as if she were a dog—throwing food on the ground to her, expecting her to pick it up, and eat it.

"The hell with you!" she snapped, and fell silent. This could be a second opportunity—not as good as the first, perhaps, but a chance to escape nevertheless.

"Little Tree," she said, and showing her bound wrists again, nodded at the piece of rabbit. She could hardly pick it up, and eat it, with her hands tied behind her. The implication was clear.

The young brave got up and came to where she sat. Motioning for her to turn around, he untied the thong, and transferred it to her booted feet, pulling the rawhide even tighter than it had been about her wrists. But her hands were free, and that was what counted.

She nodded to Little Tree, and reached out for the bit of rabbit. The brave started to move away, to return to the fire. He paused. Leaning forward he again took hold of the doeskin jacket she was wearing, fingering it fondly.

At once he decided he should have it, and grasping the garment by one sleeve began to tug. Fortuna resisted briefly, and then concluded there was little point in doing so. Slipping her arms free of the jacket she surrendered it to him, alert each passing moment of time for the opportunity to escape that she awaited.

A grunt of surprise came from Little Tree. Removing the jacket had revealed the skinning knife hanging at Fortuna's side. Moving quickly, the brave bent down to yank it from its sheath.

Fortuna was suddenly aware that the moment to act was at hand, that she would never be afforded another chance to get away from the Indians. Rocking back, she raised her legs, and drove both booted feet into the brave's belly. As the Indian went staggering back into Red Band, she hurriedly withdrew her knife, slashed the thong binding her feet together, and sprang upright. Snatching up her jacket, dropped by Little Tree, she charged straight at the two renegades, who were endeavoring to recover their balance, and get clear of the fire into which they had stumbled.

Rushing in on the pair Fortuna lashed out with the jacket, striking Little Tree across the face, causing him again to collide with his partner. Hesitating then only long enough to snatch up her pistol that Red Band had laid on the ground nearby when he started to eat, Fortuna ran to the horses, a dozen strides distant.

Yells went up from the braves. They had recovered themselves, and would be at her heels in only seconds. She reached the sorrel, turned to snap a shot at the Indians. In almost that same moment, it seemed to her, a rifle cracked from somewhere off to her left. Dirt, ashes, and smoking firebrands spurted up as a bullet drove into the center of the fire.

Fortuna was in the saddle as the braves halted dead in their tracks. A second shot broke the late afternoon hush. One of the renegades yelled in pain, which Fortuna did not know, or care. She was spurring the sorrel off into the shadows, and away from the clearing as fast as possible.

CHAPTER 16

He was pushing his horse too hard, Luttrel realized, and immediately slowed the big bay, and brought him down to a trot. It seemed he should have caught sight of Fortuna West by then, he thought, but the band of thick brush bordering the creek could have something to do with that. It did seem to him that he would have had a glimpse, however brief or distant, of her by then, however.

But when a man was dealing with an extraordinary woman of such fierce determination as Fortuna West none of the usual rules applied. She would be traveling fast, and after her experience with the Gabe Ramsey party, and from all indications, a run-in with some Indians, she would also be moving carefully.

But like it or not the lady lawman would be needing help. With no supplies, and in a part of the country where settlements were few, and days apart, Fortuna would have to depend on the land for food and fire at night for warmth. Whether she had the necessary self-reliance to provide for herself under such bleak circumstances was a question Ben Luttrel could not answer.

The day wore on, dry, and with a sort of breathless quality to the air. The sky was almost clear, showing only a few streaky clouds. There would be wind, Luttrel thought, remembering similar conditions from the past that had led up to a blow—quick, but stiff gusts now and then that stirred the trees and brush, and caused the purple-crested grass on the flats to whip violently back and forth. He could expect it about dark.

Around the middle of the afternoon as Ben was off the bay making certain he was still on the right trail by searching out the tracks of Fortuna's horse, he came to attention when shouts broke the quiet. They were men's voices, and came from the west side of the creek a short distance ahead. It seemed unlikely that the yells would have anything to do with Fortuna West, but Luttrel, a solid, straight-thinking man, was one who never took anything for granted, and mounting, rode on in the direction of the voices.

Almost at once his probing glance caught motion. It was in a clearing some fifty yards or so away. He halted. An instant later a figure spurted past his vision. It was Fortuna West! She was apparently fleeing from someone not yet in his line of sight. Jerking his rifle from the saddle boot, he spurred the bay and sent him plunging on into the tangle of brush.

Two Indians suddenly appeared in the clearing. One was wearing only a breech cloth, the other clad in drawers, and with a red rag about his head to hold his hair in place. Fortuna had run afoul of more renegades—and was endeavoring to escape from them.

Luttrel brought up his rifle for a quick shot. At that moment Fortuna fired at the pair, missing, but bringing the renegades to a halt. Ben triggered his weapon. The bullet drove into the fire in front of the braves, sending up a shower of sparks and ashes. Luttrel swore at his haste, which caused him to miss also, but the shot served to tell the pair that the woman was no longer alone.

One of the Indians—the one with the red band around his head—abruptly wheeled, snatching up a rifle that was leaning against a nearby tree. Half crouched he looked around warily. The other brave had ducked back, and was now hidden from view by the brush. Fortuna West apparently had ducked into the growth on the opposite side of the clearing, and was hidden also.

She would be realizing she was safe now from the renegades, and probably wondering who her benefactor could be. The brave with the rifle, still hunched low as if to make as small a target of himself as possible, started slowly across the open ground toward Fortuna. Luttrel brought up his weapon, sighted carefully down its barrel, and squeezed off a shot.

The brave jolted and came to a stop. For a long breath he hung there, poised, motionless, as if preparing to run. Then abruptly he toppled to one side, and lay still.

Grimly remembering there was still another brave, Luttrel urged the bay on for another dozen yards in the direction of the clearing and halted. Dropping quietly from the saddle, he secured the horse to a tree, and then, rifle ready, began to thread his way through the undergrowth. Out of the saddle, and no longer having that high point of vantage, he could not see into the clearing, but the thin twist of smoke rising from the fire effectively served as a guide.

A faint rustling in the brush brought Ben Luttrel around fast. Instinct caused him to rock to one side. A lean, dark figure, teeth bared into a mirthless grin, knife raised to strike glittering in his hand, surged out of the close-by brush.

There was no chance to use the rifle. Luttrel could only jerk back, avoid the slashing blade, and lash out blindly with his fist. The blow caught the Comanche somewhere in the body. Not effective, it did stall the brave briefly, and throw him off balance.

But with the quickness of a striking snake, the brave recovered, and whirling, threw himself at Luttrel. The tall rider dropped his rifle, useless at such close quarters, and caught the wrist of the hand holding the knife as it once again made a vicious swipe at him.

The Indian in close, face distorted with hate, eyes bright, lips still parted, muttered something between heaves for breath. Luttrel, knowing he was engaged in a struggle for life, uttered no sound. For a long minute the pair stood toe to toe, swaying back and forth as they fought for control of the knife.

Suddenly Luttrel felt himself going over backward as the Comanche threw his weight against him. His heel caught against something, a root or a partly buried rock, when he attempted to check his fall. Holding tight to the brave's wrist, he went down into the brush dragging the Indian with him.

For several moments they thrashed about, each struggling to gain control of the knife. Abruptly the brave wrenched free. Luttrel instantly rolled to one side, came up hard against a resisting bush, reversed himself, and endeavored to regain his feet. By that time the Comanche was upright. Knife poised to strike, he rushed in.

Luttrel saw death coming. His hand swept to his side, came up with the pistol holstered there. He fired without any conscious effort to aim— knowing at such close range he could not miss. The heavy .45 bullet drove into the brave, striking him in the chest, and hurling him back into the brush.

Sucking hard for wind, Luttrel drew himself to his feet and waited quietly while the echoes bounded and gradually faded among the trees. There could be more Comanches. He had seen only two, but that was no guarantee they were alone. The party he'd seen earlier with what he assumed was Fortuna's pack horse had numbered nine; could these two have been members of the same bunch sent back to trail and capture the woman? It was possible, he had to admit.

Luttrel remained motionless in the depths of the brush for a long five minutes, and then—but with the pistol reloaded, and ready in his hand—stepped to where the brave lay crumpled. A young man, Ben saw, but he'd been a lithe, powerful one. Apparently he'd engaged in a fight at some earlier time that day, or the one before, as the left side of his face was swollen, and there was a cut above his high cheekbone.

Luttrel, satisfied he had no more to fear from the brave, continued on through the rank growth to the clearing. He'd heard no more sounds, reckoned there had been but the two Comanches involved in capturing the tall, redheaded woman.

Coming to the edge of the open ground, he halted and again waited out a few minutes while he made certain his conclusion that there were no more Indians lurking about was correct. When this became apparent, he stepped into the clearing, and turned his attention to the side to which he'd seen Fortuna West running.

"Everything's all right!" he called. "It's Luttrel. I've taken care of the redskins."

There was no response. Frowning, Ben crossed the open ground, and coming to its end saw the two hobbled ponies waiting beneath a tree. They would be the ones the renegades were riding; where was Fortuna's mount?

Stepping up to the ponies, he studied the ground.

There had been three horses, he saw. It became clear then what had happened. While he was having it out with the braves, Fortuna had taken advantage of the diversion, got to her horse, mounted up, and made a run for it.

She could not have known that it was a friend taking a hand in saving her; she probably thought it another band of renegade Indians bent on taking her away from the pair who had made her prisoner. Or maybe she figured it was another party of saddle bums like Gabe Ramsey and his two partners. At any rate Fortuna had seized the opportunity presented her, and hurried on.

Luttrel swore wryly, and taking out his knife, cut the hobbles restricting the Indian ponies, and then made his way back to his own horse, recovering his abandoned rifle as he did. He had caught up with Fortuna—only to fall behind once more, thanks to the renegades who had been holding her.

CHAPTER 17

Fortuna rode hard and recklessly through the brush bordering the stream. She'd not head out across the flats, as she'd planned to do earlier, but keep in the thick growth at least until full dark so as not to expose herself in the event she was being followed.

But she would not waste any more time than she felt absolutely necessary in evading whoever it was that had enabled her to escape from Little Tree and the squat brave wearing a red rag about his head. She hadn't given much thought as to who it could have been, simply jumping to the conclusion that it was another party of renegade Indians or outlaws such as Gabe and the two friends of his she'd been forced to use her gun on. Other than those possibilities who else could it have been?

Assuredly not Red Pearson and the pair with him. They were somewhere ahead of her, she was positive, riding steadily for the Mexican border. Although they were reasonably sure no one was following them, they'd still lose no time in reach-

ing the sanctuary that crossing the line between
the United States and Mexico would afford.

Fortuna allowed the sorrel to slow his run, and
then brought him to a stop. Twisting about, she
listened into the closing night for sounds of riders in pursuit. She could hear nothing but the
low whistling of the wind in the trees and brush
as it gathered strength.

If someone had followed her she had apparently shaken them, Fortuna guessed, and now
with night coming on it would not be difficult to
stay beyond reach; she'd not halt and make camp,
but keep moving as long as practical. This would
put her that much farther ahead of anyone dog-
ging her trail as well as make up for the hours
lost while she was a captive of the Indians. But it
was still too light for her to head out across the
flats. It was best she continue under cover of the
brush until full dark.

Stirring in the saddle to relieve her tired
muscles, Fortuna put the sorrel into motion once
more. She had learned in these past days just
what Frank meant when he'd complained of being
"saddle beat." It had to do with an aching back, a
stiffness of the legs and neck, and arms that were
so heavy that it even pained to let them hang
idly at the sides. It all came from being continu-
ously in a saddle, hour after hour, for days at a
time with little or no rest.

A rabbit shot out from under the hoofs of the
sorrel, startling both him and Fortuna. She smiled
tightly, again changing position on the inflexible

leather hull. There was no need to be jumpy, she told herself; so far she had managed to hold her own and keep going despite renegade Indians and lustful saddle bums.

All at once a wave of anger went through her. Damn Red Pearson and those outlaw pals of his anyway! If it wasn't for them—the damned back-shooting killers—Frank would be alive, and she certainly wouldn't be out in the wilderness dodging braves and trail tramps, while she struggled to do the job of a lawman, and stop Pearson and the others before they could escape the law by ducking over into Mexico.

A gust of wind caught at Fortuna's hat, all but whipping it off and carrying it away. The blow was getting stronger, for sure—and she was noticing her hunger more. She wished now she had that bit of rabbit Little Tree had thrown to her back in the clearing; it would taste mighty good once the dirt was brushed off.

The band of brush began to thin. Fortuna realized the stream was making a wide curve to the east. She halted and glanced about, idly rubbing the place on her neck where Gabe's bullet had scorched a path. It was as dark now as it would get, and she reckoned it was safe now to strike out across the flats—at least as safe as it ever would be—and get to the road she believed the outlaws would be taking. Just how much farther that would be Fortuna had no idea, but it seemed to Fortuna that El Paso couldn't be too distant now.

Cutting the sorrel hard right, she rode him through the stirring, swaying brush out onto the open ground to the west. At once she was aware of the wind's true force; riding within the trees and dense undergrowth there had been protection from it; now with all that behind her there was nothing to break the harshness of the blow.

She winced as particles of sand stung her face, and loosening the bandanna she was wearing about her neck, Fortuna drew it up over her mouth and nose, and pulled her hat lower, leaving only a narrow space for her eyes. The sorrel, too, reacted. Seemingly bracing himself, he dropped his head and continued on.

An hour later, with the wind heavily laden with particles of sand and dust and steadily becoming stronger, Fortuna drew in behind a thin mesquite. She wasn't sure how much longer the sorrel, or she, could take such punishment. They must reach shelter of some kind—a deep arroyo, a stand of trees, a hut, abandoned or otherwise, where they could get out of the buffeting, stinging blasts—soon.

Coming off the saddle she took one of the rags from a pocket, poured a small quantity of water from the canteen upon it, and moving to the sorrel's head wiped his lips and nostrils and cleaned the accumulated sand and dust from his eyes. Turning back she treated herself to a swallow from the container, and then hanging it in its place, climbed once more into the saddle.

Adjusting the bandanna over her face, Fortuna,

reluctant to head again into the fierce wind, raked the sorrel with her spurs and moved him out from behind the poor shelter the mesquite had offered.

She had no idea of time, or where she might be; she could only hope that she had continued in the right direction for the El Paso road. There was no sure way to determine anything. Overhead the sky was obscured by sweeping layers of brownish sand and dust, and at ground level, had there been any familiar landmarks with which she was acquainted, none would have been visible to her. She was surrounded by a dark, shifting wall that cut her off from the outside world, leaving her with no choice but to press blindly on and hope that she had not gotten turned aside, or around, but was still proceeding in a southwesterly direction.

Eventually Fortuna was forced to halt, and she did so behind a low bluff that offered only a minimum of protection. But it helped; both she and the sorrel were near exhaustion from fighting the blustering wind, and even a poor place to rest was welcome.

She remained there for a good two hours, hoping the windstorm would pass, but it did not, and seemed in fact to grow even worse, and so once again after clearing the sorrel's nostrils, eyes, and moistening his lips, she rode on.

A time later she came to a deep arroyo with fairly vertical walls. Turning down into it she crossed to its far side where the blow could not reach her and halted. Furtive motion a few yards away in the drifting pall caused her to drop a hand to the pistol at her hip, but shortly after she saw it was only a wolf, or a coyote—in the haze she couldn't be sure which—also seeking shelter.

Repeating the previous pattern, Fortuna rested for about two hours and then moved on. Eventually the storm would end, she knew, and when it did she wanted to be as near the road to El Paso as possible. More than likely Pearson and his friends had holed up somewhere along the trail they were following to wait out the blow, and so by continuing, her chances for getting out ahead of them and waiting would be greatly improved.

The water in her canteen was getting low, she saw when she'd cleaned the sorrel and made ready to move out, but it was not being wasted. She was completely dependent on the big red horse, and it was important that he be kept in as good condition as possible to buck the punishing, screaming wind.

Fortuna had noticed her own weariness when she drew herself into the saddle, but had ignored it just as she did the hunger clamoring within her, and pointed the gelding once more into what she believed was the southwest. She had been careful to keep directions straight in her mind, and not get them confused.

If this happened, well, it would be a bit of damned bad luck—but it would not alter her determination; she'd set herself straight, and head again for Mexico, and if it developed that Pearson and the others had already crossed over the border, she'd simply go on, track them down, and either force them to accompany her back to the United States—or kill them.

Fortuna gave that thought as the sorrel plodded woodenly along through the swirling dust and sand. Kill them? Kill three more men? She could—and she would. The ability had become an accepted fact in her mind. And Pearson, Tom Benjamin, Ike Stringer—none of them deserved to live! They had wasted the life of a good man—of her husband, a man who had meant everything to her—and she would see that they paid for it.

Tired to insensibility, Fortuna realized only vaguely that the sorrel had halted, that the buffeting of the wind had decreased. She raised her head wearily. Pushing the brim of her hat a bit higher, she brushed at her eyes, and stared on beyond the gelding's pricked ears.

A band of trees and brush was directly in front of her. A deep sigh slipped from her crusted lips. She had reached a shelter of sorts—a place where she could get away from the choking, hammering blow.

Urging the sorrel on she entered the first outcropping of brush and continued slowly on, aware of the horse's nervous anxiety. A few moments later she had an explanation when a strip of silver loomed up, ghostlike, in the dusty, turbulent gloom. A creek. The gelding had smelled the water.

Halting on the banks of the stream, one about the same size as Sulphur Creek, Fortuna let the sorrel slake his thirst, and then dropping back, halted among the cottonwoods and other growth. Picketing the horse where he could graze, she settled down—cold and hungry, but too worn to really notice or care—and soon fell asleep.

Morning came only moments later, it seemed to Fortuna. Stiff, aching, her hunger increased, she got to her feet, and thankful the wind had finally died, stamped about and swung her arms vigorously to restore circulation and warmth. She could build a fire, she supposed, and while there was nothing to cook it would relieve the discomfort from the cold.

Deeming the effort worthy, Fortuna began to move about, collecting dry leaves and dead limbs from beneath the trees and brush. A sufficient amount in her arms, she started to turn back and paused. A thin streamer of smoke was climbing lazily up into the sky from somewhere only a few yards downstream. Dropping the wood, Fortuna moved cautiously to the edge of the undergrowth, and put her attention on the source of the smoke.

It was a camp—no more than twenty-five feet away. Three men—and the one standing near the fire warming his hands while the two others busied themselves with cooking chores was Red Pearson.

CHAPTER 18

"Ain't that damned Arbuckles ready yet?" Pearson growled irritably, hunching near the fire.

Ike Stringer shook his head. "Ain't had no chance to boil yet—but it won't be maybe more'n a couple of minutes. Damn it, you could give us a little help. Me and Tom didn't sign on in this little fandango to do the cooking!"

Pearson shrugged, straightening up. "Ain't but one coffeepot and one spider. Sure don't need three men to tend them."

"Expect you could rustle up some more wood, keep the fire going—"

Pearson, hands thrust deep into his pants pockets, spat and glanced about. "Hell, there's plenty of wood right handy. We ain't going to be here long, anyway, now that sonofabitching wind's quit."

Benjamin, stirring a concoction of chunked dried meat, sliced potatoes, and beans left over from the previous day's meal—all watered down—nodded.

"That sure suits me. Like I've done said, we

can't get to Mexico none too soon. . . . This here poor man's stew's about ready."

"Coffee's boiling, too," Stringer said, reaching for a tin cup.

Pearson dropped again to his haunches, and taking one of the cups, waited while Stringer filled it. Then, rocking back on his heels, Red took a long swallow of the steaming black liquid and swore gratefully. Setting the cup aside he selected a plate, laid a piece of the now hard bread on it, and then covered it with stew spooned from the frying pan.

Benjamin, already at work on his portion of the mixture, paused. "There ain't no bread left. Fact is we're damn nigh out of everything. Grub didn't go as far as we figured."

Pearson took time from his eating for another swallow of coffee. "Won't matter. We ain't far from El Paso now—just can't be. Like as not we'd be there now if we hadn't holed up out of that sandstorm."

"You figure we're really that close?" Stringer wondered.

"Sure do. Us sort of cutting out across the flats like that cowhand told us saved us plenty of miles."

"If we didn't get turned around and headed wrong," Benjamin said doubtfully.

Pearson shook his head, chewing for a bit on a piece of meat. "We didn't. I ain't one to lose my bearings and get my directions crossed up. When the sun raises behind you, you know you're headed west."

"What's this creek we wound up on?"

Pearson frowned, scrubbed at the stubble on his jaw with the back of a hand. "Ain't sure, but I've got a hunch it's the Pecos—or a creek running off it."

"Ain't hardly big enough for the Pecos, from what I've heard," Benjamin said. "And it sure can't be the Rio Grande. It's the one that goes down and run betwixt us and Mexico."

"Know that—and we ain't far enough west to be on the Rio Grande. Anyway, what the hell difference it make what it's called? We'll just follow it on down to where that road to El Paso crosses it—then we'll know exactly where we are."

Ike Stringer helped himself to more of the stew, and refilled his cup with coffee. Reaching then for their last bottle of whiskey—one less than half full—he added a small amount to the liquid in the cup.

"Getting low on liquor, too," he muttered. "I'm getting a hunch we maybe misfigured this here little sashay for sure."

"One thing for damn sure," Pearson snapped, "we ain't running short of your bellyaching! I'll be mighty glad to get to Mexico just so's I won't have to listen to you no more."

"Can hand over my seven thousand dollars right now, and I'll take off on my own," Stringer said tautly. "I sure ain't married to you—either one of you, in fact!"

"Hell—you'd never get to Mexico," Red said, with a wave of his hand. "You'd get yourself lost, and starve to death somewheres out—"

"I was looking out for myself plenty of years before I seen you," Ike declared hotly.

Pearson, bypassing his half-filled cup of coffee, took a drink of whiskey direct from the bottle.

"Maybe so," he said, "but you was like a lost sheep as I recollect. And it was me that got you going in the right direction. Ain't that so, Tom?"

Benjamin shrugged. "I ain't taking sides in this, Red. Damn fool talk, anyway. What I'd like to get settled is what me and Ike are getting for our share. You told us we'd divvy the gold three ways. Well, that five thousand you was talking about for Ike and me sure ain't splitting it three ways even!"

Red Pearson smiled. "Said I'd think about that, didn't I? Well, I still am, and I've just about made up my mind."

"A deal's a deal, Red," Stringer pointed out coldly. "And a man sure ought to stand by one when he makes it."

"I ain't said for sure yet I wasn't going to. You jaybirds've gone and got yourselves all riled up over nothing. . . . Dump some water in that pot, and get it to boiling again, Ike. I can use another cup of Arbuckles before we pull out."

Wordlessly, Stringer took up a canteen lying nearby, and poured a quantity of its contents into the fire-blackened coffeepot. Resting it on the rocks grouped about the now smoldering coals, he added wood and drew back as the flames leaped up.

"Well, then, let's settle it right here and now," he proposed curtly. "I want what's coming to me—a full third. That's what you promised, Red—a third."

Benjamin nodded. "You said yourself we was close to El Paso where we aim to cross over. Can't see no reason for you to hold off any longer. Just might be something'd happen to you, and we'd lose the whole kit and kaboodle."

"Happen? What could happen to me?"

"Texas Rangers, for one thing. We could run into a couple of them that'd take a notion to go through our gear. You'd find it mighty hard to explain twenty thousand dollars in new gold in your saddlebags—and us heading for Mexico."

"And you could get yourself in a squabble with some jasper, and get shot up—or maybe robbed by a bunch of them Mexican *bandidos*."

"We split up that twenty thousand now, it just maybe'd mean we wouldn't lose it all if something went wrong. If just one of us got away he'd have enough to keep us all going for a spell."

"Tom's right," Stringer declared. "It's risky as hell—you carrying all of them double eagles. Now, I'm right willing to settle for sixty-five hundred dollars' worth if you'll do it now."

"That ain't quite a third," Benjamin said, 'but I'm willing, too."

Pearson got to his feet, and stared off across the empty land toward the low hills far to the east. In the steadily growing sunlight the red in his beard showed clearly despite the dust and sand that had powdered it.

"If I didn't know better I'd say you boys ain't trusting me no more," he drawled.

"It ain't that," Benjamin protested, "it's just that we—"

"Tell you what," Pearson cut in, hand dropping absently to his side and coming to rest on the butt of his pistol. "I figure it'd be best for me to hang onto the gold till we get real close to Mexico, then divvy it up—sixty-five hundred a piece to you. Six thousand five hundred dollars in spanking new gold double eagles! That sound good enough?"

"I reckon so," Benjamin said, his features clouding at the seemingly innocent move Pearson had made to his gun.

"All right then, let's get to moving. I figure it'd be smart to push the horses hard, get to El Paso fast as we can."

Stringer, silent for the past few minutes, brushed at his mustache doubtfully. "Them nags ain't in no shape to be rode hard. We'll run them right into the ground if we ain't careful—then we will be in a hell of a fix. There ain't no place around here where we can get horses far as I can see, excepting El Paso."

"And we ain't even sure how far it is to there," Benjamin added. Pearson's offhand move toward his weapon still troubled him. "Red, you ain't thinking of using that hog-leg of your'n on Ike and me, are you?"

Pearson looked surprised and then laughed. "Now, why in the hell would I want to do that?" he asked, coming full around.

It was Stringer, not Benjamin, who supplied the answer. Pearson's suggestive move had not escaped him either. Narrow features cold, light eyes partly closed, he faced Pearson calmly.

"You could keep it all—the whole twenty thousand. There wouldn't be no divvying up to do."

Red shook his head. "Was I aiming to do that I'd done it a long time ago—"

"You would maybe unless you sort of wanted us along to side you till you got to the border."

Pearson turned his head aside and spat. "Well, I ain't thinking of doing no such a'thing," he stated in an aggrieved tone, "and you damn well know it! Hell, we're partners! You'll get your share when the right time comes. Now, what do you say we cut out all this palavering, load up and get humping. The sooner we reach El Paso, the—"

Red Pearson's words broke off abruptly. His eyes widened in surprise and then narrowed. "Well, I'll be a sonofabitch," he muttered. "Would you look at who's come calling!"

CHAPTER 19

Crouched low, well hidden in the underbrush, Fortuna watched the outlaws. It occurred to her in that moment if she had reached the trees and ragged growth only a short distance below where she had, she would have blundered straight into Pearson's camp. As it was she was within easy speaking distance, but thanks to the howling sand and dust-laden wind, they had not been aware of her arrival.

Anger was beginning to stir, to mount again in Fortuna as she stared at the outlaws. Here at last were the men who had killed her husband—not in a fair shoot-out, but in cold-blooded murder. These were the ones responsible for her being there, for all the fear, and strain, and hardship she'd endured; now they would pay for all of it, for Frank's murder, for what they had put her through.

It wouldn't be easy—she was aware of that. All were hardcase killers, and would fight to the end knowing that if ever brought up before a judge they would hang. Too, they would consider her a joke when she confronted them, and try to laugh her off.

Let them try—it would be the last thing they ever did. The plan of making prisoners of them was no longer a part of the scheme. She would exact punishment there and then—shooting them all three down where they stood. It was what they deserved, and nobody would ever fault her for doing it.

And there would be no hesitation when the moment came to kill. There had been a time, days ago, when the question whether she could kill a man was in her mind, and doing so was something she'd hoped to avoid, and never be forced to face up to. But the moment of truth had come and she had found it almost easy to trigger her weapon, knowing as she did that the man at whom it was pointed would surely die.

Fortuna understood now the cool arrogance of the gunfighters she'd had occasion to meet—men who had killed four or five or perhaps a dozen opponents in shoot-outs. Other than the constant vigilance in their eyes they were no different from others. Once that first time was over, Frank had said when they discussed the subject, the rest came easy. Had he killed men? She'd never given the question thought until that day.

"I'd as soon not answer that," he'd replied. "And I doubt you want me to."

She'd decided then that she really didn't want to know, but the quiet way Frank had evaded responding to her question, the respectful manner in which all men—outlaws, killers, decent citizens, and other lawmen—treated him was pretty much an answer in itself.

Red Pearson's harsh laugh broke into her thoughts, and sent a fresh roll of anger coursing through her. She could catch only a word now and then of their conversation, but Pearson appeared to be impatient to get moving again, for Mexico, she assumed. Whatever it was they had cooked smelled good. The odor of coffee, too, was in the air, and both set hunger pangs to gnawing at her insides once again.

Go on—get done with it! The impulse pushed relentlessly at Fortuna. *Now is the time to make your move—to kill them!*

It was true. The outlaws were off guard, and while still wearing their pistols and knives, surprise on her part would serve as an effective weapon in her favor. All she need do was drop back deeper into the brush skirting the creek so that she could get a few yards nearer the outlaws, and then, pistol ready, step out into the open and confront them.

Then what?

Fortuna's mouth tightened. The first one of them to show a sign of resisting—she would shoot down. The remaining two would likely go for their weapons in that moment, but she would have the advantage as her pistol would be out and leveled. Shoot again, and as before aim to kill. It would be easy to get off two quick, accurate shots before the outlaws could draw their weapons.

And that would end it. She would have avenged Frank's murder, and that of Luke Coleman—and Zeke Tyler—although the latter would be only coincidental since he was a double-crosser who had swung over and aligned himself with the outlaws. She would need only to load the bodies across their saddles, take possession of the gold, and head back for Whitehill.

Chances were she could rid herself of the bodies when she got to Mulehead, and thereby save having to tote them the entire distance home. In such hot weather the corpses would start to rot fast, and it would be smart to get them off her hands as soon as possible. A shiver passed through Fortuna at her callousness. It was a sickening matter to be discussing with herself, but hauling the outlaws' bodies back was necessary; the law must have proof that justice had been done.

Fortuna fixed her attention on the men. Some kind of an argument had sprung up between Red Pearson and his partners. She caught the word gold once or twice, and reckoned they were quarreling over it.

After a bit one of them filled the coffeepot from a canteen, and set it back over the fire. Adding some wood, he looked up at Pearson.

"Well, let's settle it right here and now," she heard him say. "I want what's coming to me, a full third. That's what you promised, Red—a third."

Satisfaction filled Fortuna's mind, tempering somewhat the hatred simmering within her. The outlaws were quarreling among themselves over the gold, and there was a good chance it would all end up in a shooting—which would make matters much easier for her. Shifting slightly to ease her muscles, she continued to watch and listen.

The argument went on. Pearson emphasized a point by dropping his hand onto the pistol at his hip. Stringer and Benjamin both took note but insisted it would be wiser to divide the stolen money then and not wait. But neither man was pushing hard, keenly aware no doubt of the subtle threat Red Pearson had made by laying his hand on the gun he was wearing.

"All right then, let's get to moving," she caught the words clearly as the outlaw's voice lifted. "I figure it'd be smart to push the horses hard, get to El Paso fast as we can."

El Paso . . . She had been right, but she had been wrong about them following the regular trail. Instead they had slanted across open country, as she had done, taking a shortcut. Only the storm, forcing them to halt and seek cover, had prevented them from getting ahead of her—perhaps even reaching El Paso where it appeared they intended to cross over into Mexico. Her pushing on in the face of the wind, while they halted, had prevented her losing them.

One of them had said it would be a mistake to ride their horses hard, that they could go down, and then would be in trouble. It would seem the outlaws knew as little about the country as she did since it was likely, they thought, that replacement mounts would be available only in El Paso, and none of them could say how far away the settlement was.

The tension seemed to be easing between the outlaws. Pearson's suggestive move toward his gun had not been lost on his two partners, and both now appeared to have accepted Red's terms—he'd hang onto the gold until they reached the border, and would then hand over their share. It was clear, however, the slightly built outlaw she believed was Ike Stringer did not fully trust Pearson. He said something about Red using his pistol on him—and Tom.

She had them straight in her mind now, Fortuna thought; the thin, wiry-looking one was Ike Stringer; Tom Benjamin, of course, would be the other.

"Now why in the hell would I want to do that?" Pearson was laughing when he asked the question.

Fortuna couldn't make out Stringer's answer, but she could guess what it was. Pearson would not have to share any of the gold if he rid himself of his partners, just as he had Zeke Tyler.

Some more was said, and tension eased even further. It was not going to come down to a shootout between them, Fortuna concluded, and dismissed the hope. It would be up to her to take care of all three of them, just as she had planned.

"What do you say we cut out all this palavering, load up and get humping—"

It was Pearson's voice, impatient and insistent.

She would have to make her move now, Fortuna realized—now, while they were all together. If she held back permitting them to separate it would shift the odds to their favor. Remaining cool, she studied them closely—where they stood, how they were wearing their guns, what cover was available behind which they could dodge—which of them would react first. It didn't matter. She intended to shoot down Pearson first, and then the others. That done, she would have her full measure of vengeance.

Vengeance . . . She'd heard Frank say a hundred different times that vengeance was wrong—that nobody had the right to take the law into their own hands regardless of cause. He'd been tempted many times, he had said, but always, in the final moments, had resisted, telling himself that only the court had the right to punish and say whether a man was to live or die. This was different. These outlaws had murdered the very man who had believed in that, and therefore were not entitled to any consideration. This time vengeance was justified.

Muffling the click of her pistol with her left hand as she cocked the hammer, holding it firm, Fortuna stepped out into the open and faced the outlaws.

CHAPTER 20

Fortuna watched surprise spread across Red Pearson's bearded face. His eyes narrowed, and he said something to the men with him that she didn't hear. Her mind, her total sensibility was centered on one thing—the three outlaws who had killed her husband, and whom she would now kill. Here at last was the moment she had lived for, the time of retribution when she would exact a penalty from them for causing all the misery and grief that had come to pass at Frank West's death, for so cruelly bringing down a dark curtain on the happy life she had enjoyed.

Her pistol leveled, Fortuna halted a few strides from the men, and waited in wary silence while Ike Stringer and Tom Benjamin slowly turned to face her.

"I'm here to kill you," she stated in a quiet, controlled voice.

Red Pearson glanced at his partners and smiled. "Boys, I expect you recognize the lady. She's that marshal's wife."

"Widow," Stringer corrected dryly.

Benjamin, lifting his hands carefully as did Red Pearson and Stringer, grinned and wagged his head.

"Yeh, we know—and she's wearing a badge! I ain't never seen no lady lawman."

"You're seeing one now," Fortuna replied curtly. Why was she wasting time on talk? Why hadn't she just gone ahead, used the gun in her hand as she'd planned? The questions troubled her.

"Badge don't count for nothing down here," Pearson said. "Maybe she's a real deputy, but she's out of her bailiwick. She ain't got no authority—"

"This is all the authority I need," Fortuna cut in coldly, moving the gun slightly.

"And you're aiming to use it on us—all three of us?"

"That's what I tracked you all the way down here for. You murdered my husband, I'm going to make you pay for it."

The slight grins had faded from the faces of the outlaws. Pearson frowned as if finding it hard to understand, or perhaps was not certain of the threat's value. Tom Benjamin lowered his hands a trifle.

"Hell—ain't no woman got that much guts—"

"She ain't by herself," Pearson stated suddenly, as if coming to a conclusion of some kind. "There's a deputy hanging around somewheres close— maybe a couple of them. No woman would've come all this way trailing us unless—"

"I'm alone," Fortuna said, her voice still quiet and controlled.

Again puzzling questions pricked at her mind. Why was she holding back? What was the point in talking? She had come to kill them, make them pay for murderously snuffing out the life of the only man who had ever meant anything to her. She had planned vengeance—here now was the opportunity she had sought—had actually created—just waiting to be taken; why was she holding back?

Was it what Frank had said about vengeance—that it was wrong for anyone but the law to exact such penalty? Fortuna felt a stir of doubt run through her as she realized she was about to do exactly what her husband had always stood against—the taking of the law into one's own hands.

But this was different, a voice within her seemed to say. She had not only the right, but a duty to rid the world of murdering scum like Red Pearson and the men with him. They were the worst sort, had doubtless killed many others besides Frank—probably were even responsible for the death of that young cowhand she had found lying on the trail—and if let live they would go on killing. There was no reason to permit that; they should be stopped—an end brought to their lawlessness.

"Now, you ain't for sure aiming to shoot us down, are you, lady?" Pearson said in a patronizing tone. A half smile cracked his lips, and his small, black eyes were hard. "You'd never get away with it."

"You're a fool if you think that," Fortuna replied evenly. "There's nobody within miles of here—and who would give a damn anyway? Killing all three of you right here will just save the hangman the job."

She was still trying to convince herself that she was in the right, Fortuna realized, and could not understand why one part of her insisted she go ahead, do as she had planned while another persistently objected. If she took the outlaws back to Whitehill they would stand trial, be convicted, and then sent to the gallows for murdering her husband; why wouldn't it be better for her to exact that penalty now, saving the law all that time and trouble?

"Well, I don't know about you jaspers," Ike Stringer began in a slow, drawling way, "but I ain't letting no damned female—"

His words broke off abruptly. Fortuna saw his hand sweep down for the gun at his side. A sort of exhilaration flooded through her. The moment in which she could purge the hatred that weighed so heavily upon her had come.

The .44 bucked in her hand. Stringer, weapon half out of its holster and coming up fast, rocked, taking a faltering step backward as the bullet struck him in the chest. A frown distorted his face as he looked down at the blood gushing from the wound, and then abruptly his legs gave out, and he crumpled into a dusty heap.

Fortuna had watched only from the corners of her eyes. She had switched her attention instantly, after triggering her pistol, to Pearson and Tom Benjamin, expecting both to go for their weapons. Neither had done so.

Pearson's arms had lowered slightly, and Benjamin had used the moment of time to take one step aside. She had but to increase the pressure of her finger on the trigger once more, and drive a bullet into Pearson, quickly aim her weapon a bit more to the left, and cut down Benjamin. It would be easy—and the job would then be done, but she heard her own voice speak out.

"Go ahead, Pearson, make your try like Stringer did. You're the one I want dead, anyway."

Both outlaws were staring at her, shocked and surprised by the swiftness of her reaction. The deadliness of purpose on her part was now clear to them, and they were fully convinced they were not dealing with any ordinary woman, but one bent on killing them, and having both the courage and the ability to do so.

Pearson's hands had risen to their original position. His features were taut, angry. "All right, lady, you're calling the shots. What's next?"

Fortuna considered the outlaw without emotion. *Shoot —shoot now!* the voice within her commanded. *Kill him, turn your gun on Benjamin, the last of the murderers, and kill him, too! Finish the job!* But again conscience, unbidden, overruled the order.

"Turn around," Fortuna snapped. "Spread-eagle

on the ground—there the other side of the fire. If either of you makes a move to draw your gun—you're dead! Move slow."

Pearson and Benjamin pivoted carefully, cautiously taking the few steps necessary to get them beyond the fire. Still using extreme care, they dropped to their knees, fell forward, and flattened themselves on the sandy soil with arms extended above their heads and legs apart.

Pearson swore, turning to one side as he sought to avoid getting a mouthful of dirt.

"Keep your face down!" Fortuna warned.

The outlaw started to protest, but thought better of it and remained silent. Fortuna, conflicting feelings of triumph and dissatisfaction battling within her, looked down at the outlaws sprawled helplessly before her. *Put a bullet in their heads!* a voice seemed to say. *Don't wait! Why go to the worry and trouble of taking them back. They could trick you, escape, and then you or some other lawman would have it all to do over again.*

"If you're going to shoot," Tom Benjamin said harshly, "then, damn it to hell—get it done with!"

At the outlaw's words the voice within Fortuna West hushed. Something seemed to snap in her consciousness, and a realization came to her that if she triggered her weapon at the killers, worthless as they were, and blasted their lives from them, she'd be no better than they.

"You'll be smart to do like Tom says," Red Pearson advised. "Long way back to Whitehill—

and you sure ain't never going to get us there—not while I'm alive."

"I'll get you there," Fortuna stated quietly. "I may have to cripple you some, but I'll get you back—maybe to some closer town where the hanging tree'll be just as high. And when they put that rope around your neck, and you start swinging, I'll be right where you can see me—laughing."

Pearson swore. "You ain't much of a woman, are you? Hell, you're worse'n any man I—"

"I'm hoping you take a long time to die—both of you. I'm hoping you choke and strangle, and kick your legs around from morning when they string you up till sundown."

Benjamin muttered something unintelligible, and Red swore deeply. Nearby on a tree a black and white woodpecker was hammering noisily as he probed for insects. Fortuna glanced at the bird, and then keeping well clear of the outlaws' arms and legs, stepped in closer and drew the weapons from their holsters. Tossing them off into the brush she fell back to where Stringer lay. Picking up the weapon he had dropped, Fortuna disposed of it in like manner.

"How long we going to keep laying here?" Pearson demanded.

Fortuna moved to the fire, and settled herself on a rock close by. "I'll let you know when it's time to get up," she replied. "Right now I'm helping myself to some of your stew, and a cup of coffee while I decide where's the best place to take you—on to El Paso, or back to Whitehill."

CHAPTER 21

Fortuna wrinkled her nose at the first spoonful of the mixture in the frying pan—a rank, salty brew the ingredients of which she could in no way fully determine. But hungry as she was she got it down—mostly with the assistance of the weak, second time around, coffee.

Staring off into the growing day Fortuna considered her best move while she worked at consuming the poor food. She had no idea of the distance to El Paso, if it were nearer or farther than Whitehill. Nor did she know if there were any other settlements in the area other than Mulehead, back to the north.

She wished again she'd made a copy of the map that hung on the wall in Frank's office. That way she would have some knowledge of where she was, and if there were other towns around where she could safely jail Pearson and Tom Benjamin until arrangements could be made to get them back to Whitehill for trial. But she had been in such a hurry that the possible need hadn't occurred to her.

As it stood now she figured she was well down in southern New Mexico—or maybe Texas, she couldn't be absolutely certain which—with a vast world of empty land all around her. If she . . .

"Come on, come on—let's get going," Pearson said irritably, squirming about to relieve his aching muscles. "Laying here's hell. I'm setting up."

"Stay like you are!" Fortuna snapped, her tone flat and uncompromising. "I'll let you know when you can move."

"You decided where we're going?"

"Not yet—"

Pearson muttered under his breath. Then, "Just like a damned woman—can't make up her mind to nothing—not one way or another!"

Fortuna's mouth tightened with anger, and then she smiled. She was enjoying the tension as well as the discomfort she was putting the two men through.

"Maybe this woman is the one who hunted you down, and will be taking you back to hang."

"I reckon it's my turn to say maybe," Pearson countered. "It's one hell of a long way from here to anywhere, and there's two of us, and only one of you."

Fortuna swallowed the last of the coffee in her cup, and tossed the container aside.

"That means nothing to me. You're both alive right now instead of laying there dead like Stringer only because my conscience wouldn't let me shoot you down, too, but it won't bother me any to kill you if you give me an excuse."

Pearson again stirred. "Oh, we believe you're a killer all right! You done proved that—but you're still just a woman, and there's aplenty you don't know about handling a couple of old heads like me and Tom."

Fortuna laughed. "I've got one answer for old heads like you—a couple of thieving, back-shooting killers—and that's a .44 bullet. Make one wrong move and you'll know what I mean."

"I reckon we savvy," Pearson said, drawling out the words. "You're just looking to put a slug into us. Now, that's where we're smarter than you think. We ain't making no moves, leastwise not till the right time comes. . . . You be interested in a deal?"

Again Fortuna West laughed. "Don't waste your breath—you don't have too much of it left," she said, voice heavy with scorn.

"Won't hurt you none to listen," the outlaw said, turning carefully to one side. Benjamin also raised his head slightly.

"Don't know what Red's got in mind, lady, but I'll sure throw in with whatever he says."

"Stay down," Fortuna warned once more. "And you can forget it, Pearson. I'm not interested."

"Well, now, you just might be," the red-haired outlaw said amiably. "You're a woman by yourself now—a widow. Tough losing your man like you did, but that's the kind of a chance you took when you hooked up with a lawman. Everybody knows that a badge-toter don't live to a ripe old age out here! If me and the boys hadn't had a run-in with him, and plugged him, sooner or later some other jasper would."

Fortuna was silent. She was in no way interested in any proposition Red Pearson and Benjamin might offer, but the outlaw seemed determined to talk, and she still hadn't decided which way was the better course to take—El Paso or Whitehill. But Pearson's words did anger her somewhat.

"Watch what you say about my husband," she said with a shake of her head. "I won't stand for you bad-mouthing him."

"Ain't aiming to, just telling you how things are with them that wear a badge," Pearson continued. "Now, this ain't no country for a woman by herself—specially a looker like you. You won't have nothing but trouble from now on. Every gent in the county'll be out after you—not to do any marrying up, but to have hisself a big time with a red-headed widow."

"Appears I can take care of myself. You're stretched out there in the dirt waiting to be hanged, while I'm the one sitting here with the gun in my hand."

Tom Benjamin muttered something to the effect that it never would have happened if they'd kept their eyes open.

"Sure, you've gone and done a big job," Pearson droned on, ignoring his partner, "but you best tell yourself, and believe it, that it was all accidental-like. Things just sort of fell your way—like drawing a pat hand in a poker game."

"Now, that's for damn sure!" Benjamin declared, speaking up. "If we'd known you was trailing us, we would've held up and took care of you—and we wouldn't be in this fix."

"Stringer tried to change that—and you both had your chance," Fortuna said coldly. "And he ended up dead. Could be things would've turned out the same if you'd tried to ambush me. Just so you won't feel too bad about it, I'm probably better with a six-shooter than any of you. Stringer, somebody said, was a fast gun. He wasn't fast enough."

"Sure, sure—but you had your iron out, and ready to shoot," Pearson said. "But that ain't what I'm getting at. You can't go on being top dog like you're figuring you are. It just won't pan out—not for a woman. What the hell are you aiming to do when—and if—you get back to that two-bit town where you're from—try to hang onto that fifty- or maybe sixty-dollar-a-month job as a lawman?

"Hell, you ain't got the chance of a snake with a roadrunner of keeping that star you're wearing. Them folks there ain't going to let themselves be the laughing stock of the whole country. Women just ain't cut out to hold a job like that.

"Now, here's what I've got in mind—and you best listen close. Forget this here taking Tom and me back to that town—"

"I'm not about—"

"Hold on—hear me out! Cards are all stacked against you, not just in getting me and Tom to wherever you figure to take us, but in this here being a lady lawman. It can't end up but one way—and that's with you being dead. You throw in with us, be my woman—hell, I'll even marry up with you if that's how you want it.

"Stringer's out of it so his split of the gold, sixty-five hundred dollars, will go to you. We'll all head on down into Mexico like the boys and me planned, and with that much money we can live high on the hog. Be even better if me and you tie up—our split would be double."

"You through talking?" Fortuna asked, rising. "If you're not, I'm sure through listening. A lot of what you've said maybe makes sense to you—but not to me. I have got one thing in mind to do, and that's get you back where they can hang you for murdering my husband, Frank. And far as that gold goes, it's covered with blood.

"Now, I want you both to get up—slow and easy. Then you're going to collect your gear, and make ready to move out. We'll be needing all the grub you've got left."

"Which ain't hardly any," Benjamin said, sighing as he came to his knees. "Figured to get some when we got to El Paso."

"Then it's the closest town—"

"No, but we ain't sure—"

"Don't tell her nothing!" Pearson snarled. "She's so damned smart, let her find out for herself!"

Fortuna shrugged. "We'll make out—live on jackrabbits and prairie dogs if we have to—"

She paused, hearing the distinct approaching

thud of a horse's hoof back in the direction where she had left her sorrel. At once she crossed the small clearing and took up a stand that put Red Pearson and Benjamin, frozen to immobility by a threatening wave of her pistol, between her and the sound.

"Hello—the camp!" a voice sang out. "Friend!"

Pearson laughed. "Lady, you done waited too long. I'm laying odds that's a friend of mine—and he'll be plenty glad to take that deal I offered you."

CHAPTER 22

Fortuna, motionless, weapon ready in her hand, waited quietly for the rider to appear. If a friend of the outlaws—and she thought it highly improbable that any acquaintance of hers would be in the area—he would never get the chance to free Pearson and Tom Benjamin, not as long as she could trigger her gun. As far as she was concerned, he would be no different from her two outlaw prisoners.

The rider came into view—a big man sitting high in his saddle. Hands raised, he advanced slowly.

"I'm Ben Luttrel," he called. "Friend!"

Fortuna recognized him at that moment. He was the man with the snakeskin hat band who had helped her out of a tight back in Gunfire. Friend of hers—or of Red Pearson? She found herself wondering as she watched him draw closer. Luttrel had sided her back in the Texas Rose saloon, doing her a big favor, but at the time he knew little if anything about her—who she was, or what she was doing. And she had remembered him from the posters in Frank's desk, as an outlaw—one wanted for murder. Odds were better than even that he would throw in with Pearson and Benjamin when he got the straight of the situation.

"Far enough!" she warned, taking no chances with the man. "Whatever you're looking for you won't find it here—so ride on!"

Luttrel brought the bay to a halt. A wry grin parted his lips. "Ease off, Deputy. Told you I was a friend."

"Whose—theirs or mine?"

Luttrel frowned. "Yours—"

"Saying it's one thing, being it's another," Fortuna commented dryly, and after a pause added: "Now, why would you want to be my friend? We've only met once before in our whole lives."

"Told you that a bit ago," Red Pearson said in a quick, triumphant way. "Said red-headed widows always found out real fast that there's plenty of men just a'pining to help them!"

Ignoring the outlaw, Fortuna awaited Luttrel's reply.

"Ain't right sure myself," the tall rider said, admiration strong in his voice. "I reckon you sort of jabbed my curiosity bone back in Gunfire—a lady deputy marshal out running down some killers! I guess I just had to see how it all come out—and maybe give her a hand again if she wanted."

"If you're half smart, Luttrel, you'll throw in

with us," Pearson said. "We've got enough gold for—"

Fortuna, pistol still covering the outlaws directly in front of her, and the still-mounted Luttrel as well, ducked her head at the pair. "You know these two?"

"Sure don't," Luttrel replied. "They the ones who killed your man—them and the one laying dead here?"

"They are. He's Ike Stringer. Decided he'd try drawing on me rather than go back to my town and hang. I'm wondering if you're any different. Saw a wanted poster on you—murder I think it was."

"Was one out on me, all right. Was cancelled. Your man was the marshal in the town of Whitehill, I was told."

Evidently Saul Harper had done considerable talking after she had ridden on, Fortuna thought.

"He was. These three, and another man, murdered him and his deputy—"

"And you just up and took it on yourself to track them down—"

Fortuna shrugged. "There anything wrong in that?"

"Nope, sure ain't—only a man don't come across a woman wearing a star every week—and one with enough sand to shoot down some jasper that got in her way."

"Can't see where that's any big thing. A gun works in a woman's hand same as it does in a man's."

"Sure, but being able to use it's something else. That's where the difference comes in. . . . It all right if I climb down off this horse? I've been pounding leather plenty hard, catching up."

Fortuna frowned. "I'd as soon you'd keep going— I don't have the time to keep an eye on you. But I reckon you can—long as you drop your gun."

The smile on Ben Luttrel's lips tightened. "Just can't do that, Mrs. West. I don't ever take it off for nobody. You'll just have to trust me."

Fortuna continued to hesitate. Pearson, hopeful, pressed his point with the tall rider.

"You interested in hearing my deal, Luttrel? Worth pretty nigh seven thousand in new gold to you! All you need do is help us shed that fool woman, and—"

Ben Luttrel silenced the outlaw with a warning shake of his head. "Not interested," he snapped, and put his attention back on Fortuna. "If it's that wanted dodger that's bothering you— forget it. I got that all cleared up more'n a year ago. It was a mistake. I'm carrying a letter from a U.S. marshal saying so."

The poised weapon in Fortuna's hand relented slightly. Luttrel took it as a sign of assent, and prepared to dismount.

She watched him step down from the bay, stretch, remove his high crowned hat, and run fingers through his hair. The signs of the windstorm still lay upon him, she saw, noting the grayness in his mustache and stubble of beard.

"You'll be needing some help getting that pair

back to wherever you're taking them," he said, glancing at the empty skillet and coffeepot, and then looking away. "Can lend you a hand."

"Haven't decided where that'll be—not sure what town's closest."

"That'll be back up the line—Mulehead. Some little jerkwater towns around but they won't have a jail, leastwise not one you could depend on. Got some rope with you? Best we tie them first off."

"Had a coil with me on my pack horse, but the Indians got him and all my gear—"

"Saw them leading a gray off. Figured he was yours. I can probably find some if I look around. You want me to do some digging in their gear?"

A feeling of relief was beginning to flow through Fortuna, easing the drag of weariness that was weighing her down. It was good to have a man there—Luttrel—taking over, helping, but she was not quite ready to concede friendship yet. She was still wary. Her encounters with men in the past few days had turned her cautious, too cautious, perhaps. Ben Luttrel seemed only to want to help; let him, but she'd keep a close eye on him.

"Go ahead."

Luttrel crossed to one of the outlaw's horses, and began to rummage about in a saddlebag. "Here's some rawhide," he announced. "It'll do fine. You aim to move out right away?"

"Soon as I can get things ready."

Luttrel nodded, and taking up the reins of the

outlaw's horses, led them to where Pearson and
Tom Benjamin were standing.

"Mount up," he directed in a positive tone. "Just
you keep your iron on them Mrs. West till I'm
done," he added, touching Fortuna with his glance.

Pearson swore, drawing himself up into the
saddle of the pinto. Benjamin climbed onto his
horse, and when they were settled, each with
hands bound securely behind his back, Luttrel
turned to Fortuna.

"What about the dead one? You toting him
back, too? Going to be mighty hot for doing that."

She had not stirred all the time Luttrel was
seeing to the outlaws, a sort of lethargy claiming
her. "Bury him. I suppose that'll be best. Anyway,
they'll believe me when I tell them he's dead."

Luttrel nodded, and taking Stringer by the heels,
dragged him off into a nearby wash where he
spent a brief time covering over the body with
brush and rocks. That done he returned to the
camp, collected and packed the outlaws' gear.

"Can move out anytime," he said, and when
Fortuna continued to remain motionless he pulled
off his hat and brushed away the sweat collected
on his forehead.

"You still wondering about that dodger?" he
asked, a wry smile on his face. Before she could
answer, he proceeded with an explanation. "Was
put out on me when I shot a fellow in self-defense,
and got jailed for doing it. Only way I could prove
it was self-defense was break out of the jail they
were keeping me in, and track down the fellow

who saw it happen, and could prove what I claimed was true.

"That's when they sent out that dodger—right after I busted out of jail. Soon's I located the fellow I was looking for I took him to the nearest sheriff's office, and had him give the straight of the shooting, then turned myself in. They cleared me of the murder charge the same day, and said they'd cancel the dodgers. Guess your man didn't get the word, overlooked it. Been a few who did."

Fortuna nodded slowly, and holstered her gun. She was not fully satisfied that Ben Luttrel was telling the truth, but having him along would be helpful. She'd simply have to keep an eye on him, just as she'd thought earlier.

Using Ike Stringer's horse as a pack animal, they rode out a short time later, heading north into the climbing, morning sun.

At her side Luttrel said: "Could be I'll be doing a mite of sleeping while we're on the move—ain't had much these last few days. It'll be a good idea to keep a close watch on your prisoners. Don't figure they can do much, trussed up like they are, but a man going to his own hanging is desperate enough to try anything."

"I'll be watching them," Fortuna replied coolly. "After going through what I did to catch them, I'm not about to let them get away now."

Luttrel leaned forward in his saddle, and looked intently at the woman. "You know, I was kind of surprised to find them two alive when I caught up with you—seeing as how handy you are with that .44."

"Was a little surprised myself," Fortuna said thoughtfully, staring out across the empty land. "Was all set to shoot them down quick as I got to them—not even give them a chance to draw and defend themselves. I figured they weren't entitled to a break.

"Stringer went for his gun, and shooting him was easy. But the others—they just stood there looking at me, sort of defying me—daring me to go ahead and shoot them, too. Hating them like I do I was burning to kill them—but somehow I couldn't. I don't know why—can't explain it. I'd figured all along to shoot them down, but—"

"You couldn't because you're not a killer," Ben Luttrel said, "and be damn glad you're not, and don't have what it takes to be one. Truth about them is that they're all walking dead men, breathing maybe, but with nothing inside them but hate and fear—and loneliness. . . . You aim to keep wearing that star when you get back to your town?"

"Doubt it," Fortuna responded, "but being busy I haven't thought much about it. Fact is with Frank—my husband—gone I've hardly thought at all about what's ahead."

"Well, just remember that things will go right on. Grass'll green up in the spring, leaves on the oaks'll turn red in the fall, and the creeks will keep rising and going down just like always. All adds up to one thing—you have to keep on living."

"I suppose, but now—it just seems there's not much reason."

Luttrel's voice dropped slightly, "I'd sure like to be a reason—"

Fortuna West drew up stiffly, a frown deepening the lines of her face. There was anger in her eyes as she considered him coldly.

"My husband's only a few days in his grave," she said in a brittle, hostile tone. "I don't want to think about anything like that—or hear it, either."

"I understand," Luttrel said quietly, jerking on the lead rope of the horse Pearson was riding that was lagging a bit. "And I respect your grief. It's only right you feel that way—but, not beating around the bush none—you're too fine a woman to wear widow weeds the rest of your life, and when you do shed them I want to be around."

He paused, waited for a response, for some small word of encouragement from the woman. She had turned away from him, was once more gazing off into the distance.

Luttrel scrubbed at the stubble on his chin. "I ain't real sure what's the best way to handle it, but I figure maybe the smart thing to do is get myself hired on as marshal of that town of yours—"

Fortuna did not look around.

"That way I can be on hand when the time comes," Ben Luttrel finished, and smiling, settled back in his saddle.

About the Author

Ray Hogan is the author of more than 100 books and 200 articles and short stories. His father was an early Western marshal and Hogan himself has spent a lifetime researching the West firsthand from his home in Albuquerque, New Mexico. His work has been filmed, televised, and translated into eighteen languages. Most recently, he has written the novels *The Renegade Gun, The Doomsday Bullet,* and *Lawman's Choice,* available in Signet paperback editions.